Lilian C. Bethel

Easy Lessons in Civil Government

arranged for individual, club, or social study

Lilian C. Bethel

Easy Lessons in Civil Government
arranged for individual, club, or social study

ISBN/EAN: 9783337390105

Printed in Europe, USA, Canada, Australia, Japan

Cover: Foto ©Andreas Hilbeck / pixelio.de

More available books at **www.hansebooks.com**

... EASY LESSONS ...

· — IN —

CIVIL GOVERNMENT

— ARRANGED FOR —

INDIVIDUAL, CLUB, OR SOCIAL STUDY.

A thorough series of Questions and
Answers on how the United States
are governed. The Functions, Powers and Limitations of the..........

NATIONAL, STATE, AND MUNICIPAL GOVERNMENTS.

Also questions on important subjects which
every one should be able to answer.

—BY—

LILIAN COLE-BETHEL.

Published by the Author, 738 E. Long Street,
Columbus, Ohio.

PREFACE.

This manual has been arranged for busy people. To study the larger works on Civil government and questions of the day, with many is impossible. Our form and system of government should be familiar to every citizen and to be able to answer intelligently many common, every-day questions, is an accomplishment to be coveted. These things I have sought to elucidate in the following pages. Some special subjects which are attracting much attention at the present time have been considered of sufficient importance to introduce here, briefly, and in a way to cover the salient points and principles enunciated. I have also arranged a list of topics for attractive programs, for clubs, and trust it may be found useful.

LILIAN COLE-BETHEL.

Columbus, Ohio.
March, 1898.

INDEX.

NATIONAL GOVERNMENT.

STATE GOVERNMENT.

"Knowledge is of two kinds; we know a subject ourselves, or we know where we can find information upon it."

"America is another word for opportunity."—Emerson.

CIVIL GOVERNMENT.

What is government?

It is the direction and control of human interests and founded upon human rights.

Name three distinct functions of government.

The legislative, executive and judicial.

Define each.

The legislative is to make laws.

The executive is to carry the laws into effect.

The judicial is to interpret and apply laws.

Name three forms of government.

Monarchy, aristocracy and democracy.

Define each.

A monarchy is a form of government in which the sovereign powers are in the hands of a single person. A limited monarchy is one in which the royal power is restricted by representative institutions of some kind. An aristocracy is a government controlled by a few persons distinguished for rank, wealth and knowledge.

A democracy is a government in which the supreme power is in the hands of the whole people and directly expressed by them. A republic is a representative democracy in which the sovereign power is exercised by representatives elected by the people. The United States and the respective states have this form of government.

The term democracy is derived from what Greek word?

Demos, meaning the people.

COLONIAL GOVERNMENT.

How were the colonies governed before the revolutionary war?

They were subject to the government of Great Britain and the power of the king.

Were all the colonies governed alike?

Each colony had a separate and distinct government, but resembled the others in form.

How were certain liberties given?

By the king granting them charters. In the chartered colonies the freemen elected the members (representative) of the lower house in its legislative department.

The powers of government were vested in whom?

A governor, a council and an assembly of representatives.

How was the governor appointed?

By the king or by such persons as had authority from the king to appoint.

How was the council appointed?

Either directly by the king or the privilege was granted the governor of the colony.

Could they make their own laws?

They could make no law contrary to the laws of England. They were granted the privilege of making some laws.

Were all the colonies granted charters?

In most of the colonies the people had but little control over public affairs, and were at the mercy of the governor.

Were the people discontented?

Yes, for many reasons. In 1663 by act of parliament the colonies were compelled to buy all their supplies in England; also manufactories in America were prohibited.

Did this oppression continue?

Yes. In 1672 the colonies were compelled by parliament to send their product of exchange from one colony to another by way of England and pay duty, or if sent direct to pay duty in America.

What act was passed in parliament in 1774 that caused such a disturbance in the Massachusetts government?

The so-called Regulation Act.

What were its provisions?

That the members of the council be appointed by the Royal governor, and that they be paid by the crown. Also that the principal executive and judicial officers be paid by the crown, and that town meetings be prohibited except for electing town officers. Other severe laws were passed at the same time.

Were these laws enforced?

Massachusetts being a chartered colony and having enjoyed certain privileges, rebelled against the new order of things. Troops were sent from England to aid in enforcing this act, and out of this political situation came the battles of Bunker Hill and Lexington.

What was the Stamp Act?

An order that stamps bought of the British government should be put on all legal documents, newspapers, pamphlets, etc.

What attitude did America have toward England in regard to the heavy tax laid upon her?

She believed that "taxation without representation was tyranny," and "that no tax should be imposed on them without their consent given directly or by their representatives."

To what did this taxation lead?

To the agitation of self-government, followed by the famous Declaration of rights, made in 1765. The feeling of bitterness was great and the agitation for home rule continued, which led to the Revolutionary war in 1775.

THE STATES GOVERNMENT.

When did the colonies become states?

They had all except two organized as states and adopted state constitutions before the constitution of the United States was adopted.

What two remained under their former charter?

Connecticut until 1818, and Rhode Island until 1842.

What colony was the first to make a new state constitution?

New Hampshire, in 1775.

"Our Liberties we prize, our Rights we will maintain."

HISTORY OF CONGRESS.

When was the first Congress held?

The first Colonial Congress, or representative Assembly of America, met in New York, Oct. 7, 1765.

Of what was it composed?

Delegates from nine Colonies.

What was the purpose of this assembly?

To oppose the stamp act and the principle of taxation without representation.

When was the next Congress held?

In 1774 in Philadelphia.

How many Colonies were represented?

Twelve.

What was done at this Congress?

The well known Declaration of Rights were drawn up and promulgated.

By what name was the body known?

The Continental Congress.

When was the Declaration of Independence adopted?

July 4th, 1776.

How many states signed it?

Thirteen. New Hampshire, Massachusetts, Rhode Island, Connecticut, New York, New Jersey, Pennsylvania, Delaware, Maryland, Virginia, North Carolina, South Carolina and Georgia.

How many members signed?

Fifty-six.

Who read the Declaration of Independence aloud in the yard of Independence Hall?

John Nixon, July 8, 1776. The same day the King's arms over the door of the Supreme Court room in Independence Hall were torn down and burned in the evening in the presence of a great crowd of citizens.

To what place did Congress remove its sittings toward the latter part of 1776?

To Baltimore.

What action was taken in 1777?

Articles of Confederation were prepared and after much discussion were passed.

When were they adopted?

In Philadelphia, July 9th, 1778, and submitted to the states.

What report came before Congress in 1785?

A committee of Congress made a report recommending an alteration of the Articles of Confederation.

Did Congress act in the matter?

No, but it was left to the State Legislatures to proceed in the matter.

How did the State Legislatures act?

The States finally agreed to have a delegated convention.

Was Congress in favor of this?

Yes. In February, 1787 it adopted resolutions in favor of a convention.

When did this convention meet?

In May, 1787.

How many states were re presented?

Seven.

Who was elected President of the convention?

George Washington of Virginia.

What was the outcome of this convention?

The Constitution of the United States was begun.

Was it finished then?

No, not until a convention of the States met September 17th, 1787.

How many states were represnted?

Twelve. Rhode Island held aloof.

How many delegates signed the Constitution?

Thirty-nine.

At the Constitutional Convention, how were the delegates appointed?

By the State Legislatures.

Who presented the Constitution to Congress?

The President of the Convention.

When did Congress direct the constitution sent to the States for ratification?

September 28th, 1787.

Was the Constitution ratified by the States by direct popular vote?

No, it was ratified by delegated conventions.

What State was the first to ratify the Constitution?

Delaware, December 7th, 1787.

How many states had ratified the Constitution before the first Congress was held under it?

Eleven. Rhode Island and North Carolina not ratifying until afterwards.

When was the new Congress held under the new Constitution?

March 4th, 1789.

Where was it held?

In New York City.

How many were present at the first Congress?

Sixty-five in the House and twenty-four in the Senate.

Upon what basis were Representatives elected in 1787?

One for every 30,000 inhabitants.

What states were represented in that Congress?

All but Rhode Island.

Where was the next Congress held?

In Philadelphia, 1790.

When did Congress move to Washington?

In 1800.

Why was Congress removed from New York?

Because the agricultural members feared the influence of surrounding commercial interests in legislation.

What was the objection to Congress continuing in Philadelphia?

Because the Southern members were afraid of the Quaker influence in urging the abolition of Slavery.

How can we amend the Constitution?

The Constitution itself makes the provision, thus: "The Congress whenever two-thirds of both houses shall deem it necessary shall propose an amendment to this constitution, or on the application of the Legislatures of two-thirds of the several states, shall call a convention for proposing amendments, which in either case shall be valid to all intents and purposes, as part of this Constitution when ratified by the Legislature of two-thirds of the several states, or by conventions in two-thirds thereof, as the one or the other mode of ratification may be proposed by Congress."

How many amendments have been made to our national constitution?

Fifteen in all.

Were these ratified by the State Legislature or State Conventions?

In every case they were submitted by Congress to the State Legislatures, for ratification.

Name three divisions of the Constitution as pertaining to goverment.

Legislative, Executive and Judicial.

"United we stand, divided we fall."

LEGISLATIVE DEPARTMENT.

What is the first section of the National Constitution?

"All legislative powers herein granted shall be vested in a congress of the United States, which shall consist of a Senate and a House of Represntatives."

Why do we have the two houses of congress?

We pattern after most of the English speaking countries having two houses. It is supposed to be a check upon hasty legislation and the interests of the people are thought to be protected since each house scrutinizes the acts of the other.

CONGRESS.   How many sessions does each congress hold?

· Two. The first cannot end until both houses are ready to adjourn. The second congress of the same session must adjourn March 4th, at noon.

What is the first session called?

The "Long Session." The second one, the "Short Session" closing the congress.

When does Congress convene?

The first Monday in December.

Can either house of Congress adjourn without the consent of the other?

Not for more than three days at a time.

If both houses do not agree about the time of adjourning what is done?

The President of the United States can adjourn them to such a time as he may think proper.

What was the longest term of Congress ever held in the United States?

The fiftieth, from December 5th, 1887 to October 20th, 1888.

What becomes of bills not passed at the expiration of Congress?

Bills run from the long to the short session, but at the expiration of the short session, March 4th, all bills not passed, perish, as the session is fixed by statute and cannot be extended.

What are some of the powers of Congress?

The Congress shall have power to levy and collect taxes, duties, imposts, etc., to pay the debts of the United States.

To borrow money on public credit.

To regulate commerce;

To establish naturalization laws and laws governing bankruptcy;

To coin money;

To promote science and useful arts;

To constitute tribunals inferior to the Supreme Court;

To declare war. To raise and support armies.

To provide and maintain a navy;

To provide for organizing, arming and disciplining the militia.

To exercise exclusive legislative action over such a district as shall contain the capitol of the United States;

To make all laws which shall be necessary for carrying into execution the foregoing powers and all other powers vested by this Constitution in the Government of the United States, or in any department, or officers thereof.

HOUSE OF REPRESENTATIVES.

How are the members of the House elected?

By the people on the basis of the population, one for every 173,901 (in 1897.)

What was the basis when the Constitution was adopted?

One Represntative for every 30,000, but each state was entitled to one Representative whether it had that number or not. Each state is still entitled to "at least one member."

How many members have we in our House of Representatives?

357 (in 1897.)

Are the members elected by the direct vote of the people?

Yes, each state elects one from each district in the State and the election always takes place in the even years.

If a state is entitled to more representatives by population than it has districts, what is done?

If the State Legislature has not made the necessary arrangements to redistrict a state that has increased in population the additional numbers are elected on a general ticket by the whole state, called Representatives-at-large.

For how long is a Representative elected?

For two years.

At what age is a person eligible to the office of representative?

"Twenty-five years, and must be a- citizen of the United States seven years."

When does his term begin?

The fourth of March in the year for which he is elected, but he does not take his seat until December unless there is an extra session.

What salary does a U. S. Representative receive?

$5,000 per annum. The salary begins on

the fourth of March next succeeding the general election.

Is this all the compensation they get?

· No, in addition they receive mileage at the rate of twenty cents a mile in going to and returning from each regular session, also an allowance of $125 for postage and stationery.

How are they paid?

From the National Treasury.

CONTESTED ELECTIONS.

How are seats contested in the House?

A person intending to contest an election of a Representative, must, thirty days after election, give notice, in writing, to the member, whose seat he expects to contest, of his intention to contest the same.

What is the nature of the notice?

It must specify particularly the grounds upon which he expects to contest.

Where are the contested cases first heard?

Usually before the Committee on Elections and they report to the House, and action is taken there.

Who pays the expenses of these contestants?

The Government pays a sum not exceeding $2,000.

In case a vacancy occurs in the representation of any state, what is done?

The Governor calls a new election and the people vote for a person to fill the vacancy.

ORGANIZATION OF THE HOUSE.

What are the officers chosen in the House?

A speaker (who is always a member of the House), clerk, sergeant-at-arms, door-keeper, postmaster and chaplain; (these are not members of the House.)

Who presides in the House?

The Speaker.

Who presides until he is elected?

The Clerk of the last session, who holds over.

What is the first thing done in organizing?

The Clerk calls the House to order and then calls the roll.

Does the Clerk know previously who the members are?

Yes, the law requires the Clerk to make a roll of the members whose credentials show they have been duly elected.

In case of a vacancy in the office of clerk,

or if he is absent or not able to discharge his duties in preparing the roll, who does it?

The Sergeant-at-arms. If neither are present, then the Door-keeper performs the office.

What vote elects?

A majority; if no one is elected on the first vote, they proceed until one receives a majority.

When elected what does the Clerk announce?

That such a person is "duly elected Speaker of the House of Representatives for the —Congress." The Speaker is then conducted to the platform and takes the oath of office.

Who administers this oath to the Speaker?

Usually the member who has been longest in continuous service. After the Speaker has taken the oath, the members from each state are called and the oath is administered to them by the Speaker.

What is the oath of office?

"I, ———, do solemnly swear (or affirm) that I will support and defend the constitution of the United States against all enemies, foreign and domestic; that I will bear true faith and allegiance to the same; that I take this obligation freely, without any mental reservation or purpose of evasion, and that I will well and faithfully discharge the duties of the office on which I am about to enter, so help me God."

After the oaths are administered, what is next done?

The members then elect the Clerk, Sergeant-at-arms, Door-keeper, Postmaster and Chaplain, each taking an oath to suport the Constitution of the United States and to faithfully perform the duties of his office.

How are the Territories represented in Congress?

By delegates. (See Territories.)

The oath of office is administered to them following the Representatives and officers.

After both houses are organized, what is done?

Each house instructs its Clerk (or secretary) to notify the other house that they have organized and are ready for business. A joint committee from both houses then waits upon the President of the United States, informing him of the organization and their being ready to receive any communications.

Following the organization, how do the members select their seats?

They draw lots for them. "The Clerk

places, in a box, a number of small balls, which are numbered, equal to the number of members and delegates. At a certain hour, previously fixed by the House, these balls are drawn by a page, the number announced and the member whose name corresponds to that number on the numbered alphabetical list, previously prepared,shall advance and choose his seat for the term for which he is elected."

How often does the House organize?

Only at the beginning of the first session of each Congress, every two years. Almost the first order of business after organizing is to adopt rules governing the House and fixing the hour for the daily meetings.

SPEAKER. What are the duties and the privileges of the Speaker?

At the hour fixed to open each day, he calls the House to order and if there is a quorum present, he calls for the journal of the last days sittings which is read and approved. He signs all acts, addresses, joint resolutions, etc. He decides all questions subject to an appeal. Being a member he can vote on all questions, his name being called last at the roll call. The Speaker has the privilege of appointing the standing committees.

What salary does he receive?

$8,000 a year.

Name some of the leading committees. Committees on Appropriations, Commerce, Rivers and Harbors, Foreign Affairs, Ways and Means, Banking and Currency, Railroads and Courts, Manufactures, Patents, Education, Labor, Pensions, Claims, Expenditures in the Departments, Enrolled Bills, Agriculture and Elections.

The Speaker must also appoint from the delegates, in addition to the committees already appointed, a delegate on the following committees: Coinage, Weights and Measures, Agriculture, Military Affairs, Post Office, Post Roads, Public Lands, Indian Affairs, Private Land Claims, Mines and Mining and two on Territories. The first one named is chairman of the standing committees.

The Speaker has the right to appoint the official stenographer of the House and the stenographer for the committees. He, also, has the power to remove them for sufficient cause. He has the privilege of appointing three regents of the Smithsonian Institute, three visitors to the Military Academy at West Point, three visitors to the Naval Academy at Annapolis, two directors of the Columbia Hospital for women two directors for the Columbia Institute for the Deaf and Dumb, and two consulting trustees for the Reform School of the District of Columbia.

Congress provides that the Speaker shall set aside a portion of the West Gallery for the use of the President of the United States and the Cabinet, the Justices of the Supreme Court, Foreign Ministers and suites and the members of their families; also, for persons admitted on the cards of members. The Southern half of the East Gallery is for the members' families.

CLERK. A part of the duties of the Clerk has already been given in the organization of the House.

What are some of the requirements of the Clerk?

After he enters upon his duties, he must give bonds for $20,000.

The salary of the officers and employes of the House, as fixed by law, are paid by the Clerk by warrants on the U. S. Treasury. He must also keep an accurate account of all disbursments out of the contingent fund of the House, monies expended, etc. He is, also, authorized to sign, during the recess of Congress, the certificates for the monthly compensation of members and delegates, also from the time a member is duly elected to the opening of the first session.

The Clerk of the House and Secretary of the Senate must advertise once a week for four weeks in some leading paper, or papers, published in the District of Columbia for sealed proposals for supplying both houses with necessary stationery.

The Clerk gives a printed order for printing and binding, or for blank books for the House, subject to the approval of the committee on accounts.

The Clerk of the House and the Secretary of the Senate are required to procure and file all reports made by each committee; these reports with all succeeding reports are bound and deposited in the library of each house.

He furnishes to members a list of official reports. He makes or approves all contracts, bargains for the performance of any labor for the House, according to the law or order of the House. He reads all messages and bills, and calls the roll of members and keeps on file all papers belonging to the House. He keeps the library of the House, where all copies of printed documents of either House are kept.

SERGEANT-AT-ARMS. What are the duties of the Sergeant-at-arms?

He is to assist the Speaker to keep order in the House.

Is he required to give bonds?

Yes. After he is elected and has taken the oath of office, he must give bonds with two or more securities, to be approved by the first comptroller of the Treasury, for the sum of $50,000, as disbursing officer of the United States.

Can a member of congress go, as security, on such a bond?

No.

With whom shall these bonds be deposited?

With the first Comptroller of the Treasury.

How are the members of the House paid?

Out of the United States Treasury, on an order drawn by the Sergeant-at-arms of the House. He must keep accurate account of the salaries and mileage of the members and delegates and pay them as above stated.

How long does he hold his office?

He continues in office, the same as the Clerk, until his successor is elected and qualified, unless otherwise removed.

Does the Sergeant-at-Arms do all this work?

No, the law allows him as assistants, one deputy, one cashier, one paying teller, one bookkeeper, one messenger, one page, and one laborer. These are all paid by the government.

The Sergeant-at-Arms of both Houses have the right to appoint the capitol police under the call of the House.

What else is the Sergeant-at-Arms required to do?

In the absence of a quorum, fifteen members including the Speaker shall be authorized to compel the attendance of those absent, the doors shall be closed and the ab-
sentees noted, who by the order of the majority shall be sent for and arrested, where-
ever they may be found, by officers appointed by the Sergeant-at-Arms, and the House
shall determine upon what condition or
fine they shall be discharged.

THE DOOR-KEEPER.—What are his
duties?

The Doorkeeper sees that the rules are
observed relating to the privileges of the
Hall and is responsible for the conduct of
his employees. At the beginning and close
of each session he must report to the House
an account of all furniture, books and public property in the various committee and
other rooms under his charge. This report
is referred to the committee on account, and
they hold him liable for missing articles.

THE POSTMASTER. What are his
duties?

He shall keep the postoffice in the Capitol for the convenience of the members,
and is responsible for the safe delivery of

their mail.

The Postoffice is open every day in the year, whether Congress is in session or not, and the Postmaster must see to forwarding all mail, if not delivered.

THE CHAPLAIN attends the opening of each day's sitting and opens the same with prayer.

THE PAGES are elected by the House, usually on the recommendation of some member, and receive a salary of two dollars and a half per day.

Can a member of either house hold any other office under the United States at the same time?

No.

Are members exempt from arrest?

Members of both houses cannot be arrested except for treason, felony or breach of the peace, during their attendance upon their respective houses, and in going to and from the meetings of Congress.

What is the title given to a member of Congress?

"Honorable."

Can a person be a member of Congress and a Cabinet officer at the same time?

No, nor can a Representative be appointed an elector, or practice in the Court of Claims. A member of Congress cannot hold an office he has helped to create.

A member cannot accept payment from a citizen for any service, except for legal services and even then the law forbids him to accept pay for obtaining pensions.

Any member found guilty of accepting bribes may be expelled or fined or imprisoned. A member cannot make a public contract under penalty of $3,000 fine.

If a member resigns to whom does he give his resignation?

To the Governor of the State.

What provision does the constitution make about members receiving titles?

"No title of nobility shall be granted by the United States, and no person holding any office of profit or trust under them shall without the consent of Congress, accept of any present, emolument, office or title of any kind whatever from any King, Prince or foreign State."

Each member and Delegate is entitled to a clerk, during the sessions of Congress, who is paid out of the contingent fund. The amount for clerk hire must not exceed $100 a month.

After the organization and the committees appointed, they then being ready for business, how is it introduced?

Usually by the presentation of bills.

What is a bill?

A form or draft of a law presented.

What is a preamble?

If there is a preamble, it is the introduc·
tory part of the document, which states
the intents and reasons of the same.

What is a memorial?

A representation of the facts presented
to the Legislature for some other body, usually accompanied by a petition.

How is a bill headed?

The style and title such as "An act mak·
ing appropriations——for the year ending
July—" is used.

What else in the form of heading?

Always, "Be it enacted by the Senate
and the House of Representatives of the
United States of America in Congress as·
sembled————."

When is a bill voted on?

It can be referred to the proper commit
tee after the first reading, amended at the
second and voted on after the third. Af·
ter the third reading the bill cannot be
amended but can be debated.

What is then done?

The vote is taken. If carried by a ma·
jority it passes. Only after a bill is passed
is the "title" subject to amendments and
that without debate.

What is done with a bill after it passes?

The engrossed bill, certified to by the Clerk is then carried by the Clerk of the House to the Secretary of the Senate, where the bill is presented with a message requesting concurrence.

If the bill passes the Senate, what is then done with it?

If it passes both houses, it is enrolled on parchment under the direction of the Clerk or Secretary of the House in which it originated and is then signed by the Speaker of the House and President of the Senate. It is then taken to the President at the Executive Mansion by the Clerk or some member of the enrolling committee to be signed. The date when presented is on the bill.

If the President approves the bill what does he do?

He writes the word "approved" on the bill and it becomes a law. It is then deposited in the state department.

If the President does not approve the measure what does he do?

Vetoes it. That is he returns the bill to the house in which it originated and upon it he states his objections, and these objections must be entered at length on its journal.

Can a bill ever become a law over the

president's veto?

It can be reconsidered and if two-thirds of the members favor it and it is thus carried in both houses, it becomes a law even over the President's veto.

Can a bill become a law without the President's signature?

Yes. If a bill is presented to him and he does not sign and return it within ten days, (Sundays excepted) it becomes a law, the same as though he had signed it. The Wilson Tariff bill was not signed by the President (Cleveland) but became a law.

If Congress adjourned and the President has not signed or returned the bills presented to him, what becomes of them?

They fail to become a law. This has been termed a "pocket" veto.

What President first practiced the "pocket" veto privilege?

Jackson in 1829.

What does the word veto mean?

It is a latin word meaning "I forbid."

In what house must bills for raising revenue "originate?"

In the House of Representatives, but the Senate may propose amendments.

Which House can impeach?

The House of Representatives has the sole power of impeachment and the Senate the sole power to try impeachments.

What rules of order govern both Houses of Congress?

Jefferson's Manual. Outside of this each house has special rules of its own.

Who reads the President's message?

The Clerk.

What are the modes of voting in the House of Representatives?

By viva voce vote, by teller vote, by ballot and by the yeas and nays.

What is the teller vote?

If the chair in deciding a viva voce vote is doubted he asks the members to rise and be counted, and if this is doubted he appoints two tellers. These tellers, or counters, are stationed in front of the Speaker's desk, and the voting members pass between the tellers, and are counted and the result announced to the Speaker.

What is the yea and nay vote?

The recorded vote. The Clerk calls the roll and each voter is recorded "yea" or "nay."

How is the vote in the House of Commons taken?

The members go into the lobby. where they are counted.

"A man's love for his native land lies deeper than any logical expression among the pulses of the heart which vibrate to the sanctities of home and to the thoughts which leap up from his father's grave."
—Chapin.

THE SENATE.—Name three functions of the Senate.

Legislative, executive and judicial.

What are the legislative functions?

To make laws with the house of representatives.

What are its executive functions?

To approve or disapprove the President's nominations of federal officers, such as judges, ministers and ambassadors; also of treaties made by the President.

What are its judicial functions?

To try cases of impeachment preferred by the house of representatives.

How are the senators elected?

By the state legislature for a term of six years. They are elected by a majority of both houses.

Who signs the senators' certificates?

The governor, under the seal of the state, and the president of the senate. It is also signed by the secretary of state.

Do all the senators' terms expire at the

same time?

No. The constitution provides that one-third of the senators shall be elected every two years, and no state shall elect both of its senators at the same time.

In case of vacancy how is the office filled?

If a vacancy occurs during the recess of the legislature, the governor makes the appointment until the legislature meets, and then they fill the vacancy.

How long does a senator appointed to fill a vacancy hold his seat?

Until the next session of the legislature elects a successor.

If the state legislature fails to elect a senator, having had an opportunity, can the governor fill such vacancies?

No.

At what age is a person eligible to the office as senator?

Thirty years, and must have been a citizen of the United States nine years.

How many senators has each state?

Two.

How many senators in all have we?

Ninety. (1897.)

When does a term begin?

On the fourth of March, on the expiration of the term of his predecessor.

What salary does a senator receive?

$5,000 per annum. He also receives, for

expenses, mileage at the rate of twenty cents a mile traveling to and from congress and one hundred and twenty-five dollars for stationery, paid from the national treasury.

Who presides in the senate?

The vice president of the United States, by virtue of his office, is president of the senate. If the vice president is unable to preside, the senate chooses one of its members to be president pro tempore.

Does the senate organize in the same manner as the house?

Not exactly. The senate chooses its new officers at the beginning of the new congress—such as secretary, clerks, sergeant-at-arms, pages, etc.

If the vice president is not present at the opening of the new congress who presides?

The secretary, until the president pro tempore is elected.

Is the vice president a member of the senate?

No; and he can only vote when the senate is equally divided; when he gives the casting vote.

Has the president of the senate the same privilege as the speaker of the house in appointing committees?

No; as he is not a member of the senate,

the committees are elected by ballot by the members.

Who administers the oath of office to the senators?

The president of the senate.

What is the oath?

The same as that taken by the representatives.

What are the duties of the secretary of the senate?

Similar to those of the clerk of the house as to the business brought before the senate.

How are the senators paid?

By the secretary of the senate. The secretary, as the disbursing officer of the senate, must, within thirty days after election, give a bond to the Unite States, with securities to be approved by the first comptroller of the treasury, for twenty thousand dollars.

How are bills passed in the senate?

The routine business of the senate in presenting and passing bills is similar to that of the house.

Is the previous question used in the senate?

No, it is not used in the senate, but it is in the house.

The president of the senate appoints

three senators on the board of regents of the Smithsonian institution; also, other national institutions are represented by senators.

Who presides over the senate in case the president of the United States is impeached?

The chief justice of the supreme court of the United States.

"Signs of nobleness, like stars, shall shine on all deserved."—Macbeth, 1:4.

EXECUTIVE DEPARTMENT.

Who is the Executive officer of the Federal Government?

Art. II of the Constitution reads: "The executive power shall be vested in a President of the United States of America."

Who is our President?

William McKinley of Ohio.   (1897.)

What are the qualifications of a President?

He must be thirty-five years of age a "native born citizen" and a resident of the United States fourteen years.

For how long is he elected?

Four years is a term and he may be re-elected.

What salary does he receive?

$50,000 a year.

Has this always been the salary of the President?

No.   In 1873 it was increased from $25,-000 to $50,000.

How is the President elected?

By the people through the electors. (See Electoral College.)

When does his term of office begin?

On the fourth of March following his election.

Who administers the oath of office to the President on inauguration day?

The Chief Justice of the United States.

Where does he give his inaugural address?

On the eastern steps of the Capitol.

What is the oath?

"I do solemnly swear (or affirm) that I will faithfully execute the office of President of the United States and will, to the best of my ability, preserve, protect, and defend the constitution, of the United States."

After a bill has passed and becomes a law, what is the duty of the President?

"He shall take care that the law is faithfully executed."

In case the President dies or the office becomes vacant, who becomes President?

The Vice-President fills the unexpired term.

Have both offices ever been vacant at the same time?

No.

How many Presidents have died while in office?

Four; Harrison, Taylor, Lincoln and Garfield.

Name the order in which the office of President is filled if vacant by removal or death?

By the Vice-President, and then by the Cabinet officers in the following order: Secretary of State, Treasurer, Secretary of War, Attorney General, Postmaster General, Secretary of the Navy, Secretary of the Interior.

What are some of the powers granted the President?

"He shall have power to nominate, and by and with the advice and consent of the Senate shall appoint ambassadors, other public ministers and consuls, judges of the supreme court, and all other officers of the U. S. whose appointments are not otherwise provided for, and which shall be established by law."

"He shall have power to fill all vacancies that may happen during the recess of the Senate by granting commissions, which shall expire at the end of the next session."

The President is Commander-in-Chief of the army and navy and the militia of the several states when called into national service.

He has power to grant reprieves and pardon for offences against the United States, except in cases of impeachment, with the consent of the Senate.

He has power to make treaties with foreign countries with the consent of the Senate

He has power to call extra sessions of Congress.

He appoints all the Cabinet officers.

He gives to Congress from time to time information concerning the state of the Union. All orders, resolutions or acts passing both houses must be presented to the President and he has the privilege of signing or not.

In order that the President may be able to carry out all laws passed in Congress, he has the privilege of appointing subordinate officers, the principal ones being called the Cabinet officers.

VICE-PRESIDENT.

Who is our Vice-President?

Garret Hobart of New Jersey.   (1897.)

What are the qualifications of a Vice-President?

The same as the President.

What salary does he receive?

$8,000 a year.

Who administers the oath of office to the Vice-President?

The retiring Vice-President in the presence of Congress, on March 4th. He takes the oath of office before the President is sworn.

What does the Vice-President do as soon as he has taken the oath?

After prayer by the Chaplain he requests the new Senators to come forward and take the oath of office.

How many Vice-Presidents have been called upon to finish out the presidential term?

Four.

Who were they?

John Tyler, 1841; Millard Fillmore, 18-50; Andrew Johnson, 1865; Chester A. Arthur, 1881.

THE ELECTORAL COLLEGE.

Are the Presidents and Vice-Presidents elected by the direct vote of the people?

No.

How are they elected?

By electors, elected by the people.

How are these electors elected?

In every Presidential election, or what is called Presidential election, each state elects as many electors as they have Senators and Representatives in Congress and each elector has one vote. For instance, Ohio has twenty-one Representatives and two Senators in Congress therefore is entitled to twenty-three electors.

To how many electors are the different States entitled?

Alabama	11	Nebraska	8
Arkansas	8	Nevada	3
California	9	New Hampshire	4
Colorado	4	New Jersey	10
Connecticut	6	New York	36
Delaware	3	North Carolina	11
Florida	4	South Carolina	9
Georgia	13	North Dakota	3
Idaho	3	Ohio	23
Indiana	15	Oregon	4
Illinois	24	Pennsylvania	32
Iowa	13	Rhode Island	4
Kansas	10	South Dakota	4
Kentucky	13	Tennessee	12
Louisiana	8	Texas	15
Maine	6	Utah	3
Maryland	8	Vermont	4
Massachusetts	15	Virginia	12
Michigan	14	Washington	4
Minnesota	9	West Virginia	6
Mississippi	9	Wisconsin	12
Missouri	17	Wyoming	3
Montana	3		

Is the Electoral College a permanent body?

No, they are elected every four years and serve only in the casting of their ballots for the President and Vice-President.

When does this election take place?

The first Tuesday after the first Monday in November of every fourth year. This is the same in all states.

Can a Senator, Representative or any person holding a position in the general government, serve as a presidential elector?

No.

Where do the Electors meet to cast their ballots?

Each state's electors meet at their respective capitols.

When does this meeting take place?

Always in each state the second Monday in January. All of the Electors meet at the same time.

What is their order of conducting the Electoral College?

The College is organized, each elector takes the oath of office. The Electors then vote for President and Vice-President. These votes are counted by tellers, when the vote has been counted, three separate lists are made of all the persons voted for as President and Vice-President and how many votes each received. These lists are sealed, signed and certified to by all the Electors.

What becomes of these three lists?

One is sent by mail, and one is sent by a special messenger to the president of the United States' Senate, and the third one is taken by a messenger and deposited with the United States District Court Judge of the district in which the Electors meet.

How are the messengers elected?

By lot in the College.

Are the Electors paid a salary?

No. But their expenses are paid by the state.

Why are three copies made?

In order to preserve the record and to provide against accident.

What if the copies should fail to reach the president of the Senate?

The Secretary of the State is notified and he sends a messenger to procure the copy deposited with the District Judge.

When are these votes counted in Congress?

The second Wednesday of February when the members of both houses meet in the House of Representatives at 1 p. m.

Who presides?

The president of the Senate.

The sealed envelopes are then opened by the president of the Senate. As these are opened all the certificates and papers purporting to be certificates of the Electoral votes are acted upon in alphabetical order of the States, and are handed to the four tellers (two from each house), and read aloud.   A list is made of the votes cast by each state and the result announced.

The person voted for as President having the highest number of votes and a majority of all votes cast is elected.

The Vice-President is elected in the same way.

Suppose no one received a majority of the votes cast?

There would be no election.

In case of no election what would be done?

The House would then elect the President and the Senate the Vice-President.

Why naturally would the House elect the President and the Senate the Vice-President?

The President represents the nation and elected indirectly by the people, next to the Electoral College, would be the Representatives, who had been elected directly by the people.   As the Vice-President is the President of the Senate, if there is no election in the College the Senate would naturally elect their own president.

How does this election for President pro-ceed?

The House takes three persons who had received the highest number of votes in the Electoral College and proceeds to ballot. The votes are taken by States and the representation from each State has one vote. A quorum for this purpose consists of a member or members each from two-thirds of all the states.

What vote in the House would then elect?

A majority of all the States.

What would be done if the House failed to elect before the fourth of March?

The Vice-President would act as President until one was elected.

How many Presidents have been elected by the House?

Two. Thomas Jefferson and John Quincy Adams.

In 1801 when the Electoral votes were counted, Jefferson and Burr on the Republican ticket each received 73 votes, a tie; John Adams 65 and Charles Pickney 65. As there was no election, the election was thrown into the House, which elected Thomas Jefferson.

In 1825 the candidates in the Electoral College received: Andrew Jackson 99; John

Quincy Adams, 84; William Crawford, 42 votes. There being no election the House elected John Quincy Adams, although he did not receive the highest vot? in the Electoral College.

Is the Electoral College the same today that it was when the first President was elected?

No. The electoral votes did not state whether the candidates named in them were candidates for the presidency or the vice-presidency. Each Elector in the College wrote two names. In the official count the candidate having the highest number of votes, providing he had a majority of all votes cast, would be declared President, and the candidate receiving the next highest was declared Vice-President. This caused a good deal of dissatisfaction; so, in 1804 the 12th amendment was made to the Constitution, which gives us our present system.

What Vice-President was elected by the Senate?

Richard M. Johnson in 1837.

How many electoral votes did Washington receive?

Sixty-nine.

How many states voted for him?

All but New York, Rhode Island and North Carolina.

MEMBERS OF THE CABINET.

Who appoints the Cabinet?

The President, and the Senate confirms.

Name the departments and when established?

The department of State, July 27, 1789.

The department of War, Aug 7, 1789.

The Treasury department, Sept. 2, 1789.

The Post-office department, May 8, 1794.

The department of the Navy, April 30, 1798.

The department of the Interior, March 3, 1849.

The department of Justice first in 1789; then June 22, 1870.

The department of Agriculture, February 12th, 1889.

What is the salary of a Cabinet officer? $8,000 a year. The Cabinet officers are considered an advisory board and each stands at the head of a department.

THE SECRETARY OF STATE. Who was the first Secretary of State?

Thomas Jefferson.

What are the duties of the Secretary of State?

He has charge of Foreign affairs and is the only officer who has the authority to communicate with other governments in the name of the President of the United States. He attends to the correspondence with the public ministers and consuls of the United States, giving them instructions abroad and takes a leading part in the negotiations of Treaties. He keeps the national archives, superintends the publication of laws, treaties, presidential messages, etc., and the proclamation declaiming the admission of new states into the Union. He is the keeper of the great seal of the United States, and affixes it to all official papers. He must keep Congress informed as to the relations between foreign countries and our own.

SECRETARY OF THE TREASURY.

Who was the first Secretary of the Treasury?

Alexander Hamilton.

What are the duties of the Secretary?

He looks after the financial interests of our country, suggests plans for creating revenue, and maintaining the credit of the United States. He superintends the collection of the revenue. He grants warrants for all money drawn from the Treasury, in accordance with the appropriations made from time to time by Congress.

He superintends the coinage, engraving

and printing of money, the National Banks, the custom house, coast survey and light house system, the marine hospitals and life saving service and is the supervising inspector-general of steam boats.

He also looks after and pays the interest on the national debt.

Though there are many in the Treasury department to carry out the work such as Secretaries, Auditors, a Register, a Comptroller, Clerk, etc., the Secretary of the Treasury has a general supervision over it all.

Through this department all money due the Government is received.

The Treasurer has in charge the receiving and disbursement of all public moneys t are deposited in the Treasury at shington and the subtreasurer at Bos- ..., New York, Baltimore, Philadelphia, New Orleans, San Francisco, St. Louis, Chicago and Cincinnati; also, the National Bank United States depositories; is trustee for the bonds held to secure national bank circulation and public deposits in national banks, etc.

What are some of the duties of a Register?

He keeps an account of all receipts and expenditures of the Government except those belonging to the Postoffice department. He signs and issues all bonds of the United States: his name is upon bonds and United States notes: his books at any time must show the financial condition of the government.

What are some of the duties of the Comptroller of the Treasury?

He is required to give his decision upon the validity of a payment to be made, to approve, disapprove or modify all decisions of the Auditors.

"The Comptroller passes upon the sufficiency of authorities to indorse drafts and receive and receipt for money from the government and upon the evidence presented in application for duplicates of lost or destroyed U. S. bonds, drafts, checks, etc."

The Comptroller of Currency has charge of the national banking system to see that the law is complied with in organizing and carrying on national banks. He sees that national bank accounts are examined by agents and makes regular reports.

He has charge of printing bank notes and delivering the same.

How many Auditors of the Treasury department?

The business of the entire Treasury department is audited by six auditors.

What are the duties of the Director of ...nt?

He has the supervision of all mints and assay officers in the U. S. and receives for adjustment the accounts of the mints and assay offices, etc.　He tests the weights and fineness of coins, etc.

What other departments of the Treasury besides these already given?

A Commissioner of Internal Revenue, who superintends the collection of duties and taxes levied by Congress.

A Solicitor of the Treasury who looks after the attempted frauds of the custom revenue.　As law officer of the Treasury department many matters are referred to him under the customs, navigation, banking and registration laws.

What is the purpose of the Bureau of Printing and Engraving?

It is where engraving and printing designs for the government are made, such as United States notes, bonds and certificates, national bank notes, internal revenue and custom stamps, treasury drafts and checks, disbursing officers' checks, licences, commisions, patent and pension certificates, etc., etc.

What is the purpose of the Bureau of Statistics?

It is where reports of trade and commerce of the country are kept.

What do the "scales" on the seal of the U. S. Treasury represent?

They represent justice, the "key" security, and the "rule" exactness.

THE SECRETARY OF WAR. Who was the first Secretary of War?

Henry Knox of Kentucky.

What are the duties of the Secretary of War?

He has charge of the military affiairs of the country; carries out the orders of the President concerning the military service; has supervision of all the estimates for appropriations for the expenses of the department; purchases army supplies and attends to the transportation of armies.

He, also, has supervision of the military academy at West Point; also, the National Cemeteries.

THE SECRETARY OF THE NAVY. What are the duties of the Secretary of the Navy?

Under the directions of the President of the United States, he has general supervision of the navy department, such as constructing, manning and equipping vessels of war?

How many divisions in the department?

There are eight departments under the heads of bureaus. Bureaus of yards and docks; equipments and recruiting; navigation; ordnance; construction, and repair; steam engineering; provisions and clothing; medicine and surgery.

The Naval Observatory at Washington is under the direction of the Secretary of the Navy.

THE ATTORNEY GENERAL.—What are the duties of the Attorney General?

He is the legal advisor and is at the head of the Department of Justice. He has the general superintendency of the United States attorneys and marshals in all the Judicial districts in the States and Territories. He represents the United States in all suits at law with the government; he gives his advice and opinion when asked by the head of any department or by the President. He examines titles to lands for the erection of public buildings, etc.

Who was the first Attorney General under Washington?

Edmund Randolph of Virginia.

THE SECRETARY OF THE INTERIOR.—What are his duties?

He has general supervision of public business relating to patents for inventions; pensions and bounty lands; the public lands and surveys; the Indians; education; rail-

road; geographical survey; the census; the
Hot Springs reservation in Arkansas; Yel-
low Stone national park in Wyoming; and
the Yosemite, Sequoia and General Grant
parks in California; the distribution of appropriations for agricultural and mechanical policies in the states and territories, etc.

THE POST MASTER GENERAL.—
Who was the first Post Master General?

Samuel Osgood of Massachusetts, appointed in 1789.

What are the duties of the Post Master
General?

He has full direction and management of
the Post Office department.

Who appoints the four Assistant Post
Master Generals?

The President with the consent of the
Senate. The Post Master General appoints all other officers and employes and
all post masters whose compensations do
not exceed $1,000. All others are appoint-
ed by the President and Senate. The Secretary controls the style of postage stamps
and envelopes made by the government.
Prescribes the rules and regulations for the
entire postal system.

With the consent of the President the
Post Master General makes postal treaties
with foreign governments.

What are some of the postal laws?

·No post office can be kept in a bar room. Every letter carrier must give bonds with security to be approved by the Post Master General for the safe delivery of mail. Letter Carriers are approved by the Post Master General upon the recommendations of the Post Master. The Post Master General may prescribe a uniform dress to be worn by letter carriers, and anyone wearing this uniform not connected with the postal service is liable to a fine of not more than $100. or imprisonment of six months or both.

SPECIAL DELIVERY SERVICE.— What are post roads?

They are thoroughfares by land or water over which mail travels. Mails must go on the fastest trains. Railroads carry mail by weight so much for every hundred pounds There are four classes of mail. First class contains written matter. Second class periodical publications. Third class miscellaneous printed matter. Fourth class merchandise. Postal cards cannot be issued by private parties.

What are the mail rates?

The letter rate is two cents for every ounce or fraction of an ounce. Periodicals, magazines, etc., are one cent a pound when sent from a registered publishing house or news agency, otherwise they are one cent for four ounces. Books are one cent for every two ounces or fraction of an ounce. Merchandise is one cent an ounce, limited to four pound packages. Circulars and printed matter in an unsealed envelope are one cent for two ounces.

SECRETARY OF AGRICULTURE.— The Secretary of Agriculture has charge of what business?

Of all public business pertaining to the agricultural industry. He has supervision over all agricultural experiment stations, that are supported by the government. He superintends the gathering and printing of all agricultural statistics and the distribution of valuable seeds, etc., for experiment and improvement of production. The weather bureau since 1891 has been under this department. The Assistant Secretary of Agriculture and Clerk of the Weather Bureau are appointed by the President.

NAME THE PRESENT CABINET OFFI-CERS, TERM, 1897 to 1901.

Secretary of State, Hon. John Sherman of Ohio.

Secretary of the Treasury, Hon. Lyman J. Gage of Illinois.

Secretary of War, Gen. R. A. Alger of

Michigan.

Secretary of the Navy, Hon John D. Long of Massachusetts.

Attorney General, Hon. John W. Griggs of New Jersey.

Secretary of the Interior, Hon. C. N. Bliss of New York.

Post Master General, Hon. James A. Gary of Maryland.

Secretary of Agriculture, Hon. James Wilson of Iowa.

DIPLOMATIC SERVICE.

Who has charge of the Diplomatic Service of the United States?

The Secretary of State.

How are our interests represented in foreign countries?

By Ambassadors, Envoys Extraordinary, Muinisters Plenipotentiary, Ministers Resident, Consuls-General, Consuls, and Commercial Agents.

How are they appointed?

By the President.

What is meant by Ambassador?

An Ambassador is a diplomatic agent of the highest rank, employed to represent officially a sovereign nation at a foreign court.

What countries are represented by U. S.

Ambassadors?

Great Britain, France, Germany and Italy.

What are Envoys Extraordinary and Ministers Plenipotentiary?

In diplomacy that is the full title of Ministers of the second grade resident in a foreign country, next in dignity to an ambassador. They act as the agents for communication and the transaction of business between the two governments.

What country sent the first diplomatic representative to this country?

France in 1778.

The whole consular service is the great factor in looking after our entire foreign affairs. We have more than twelve hundred persons connected with our government, located in the important cities and towns of the world.

In how many countries are we represented?

Forty-three.

How many countries are represented in this country?

Thirty-nine.

How are they supported?

By a salary paid by the country sending them.

How are they recognized in the country

to which they are sent?

They are known by their credentials. These credentials of foreign ministers are presented to the Secretary of State and examined.

JUDICIAL DEPARTMENT.

What is meant by the Judicial Department?

The Constitution says: "The Judicial power of the United States shall be vested in one Supreme Court, and in such inferior courts as the Congress may from time to time, ordain or establish."

How are Federal Courts divided?

Into three classes.

The Supreme Court, the Circuit Court, and the District Court.

When was the first Supreme Court held? In 1790 in New York.

How many members of the Supreme Court?

Nine. Each Judge is also presiding judge of a circuit court.

How many in the original Supreme Court?

Six.

How are they appointed?

By the President and confirmed by the Senate.

How long do the judges of both the Supreme and Circuit Courts hold office?

For life or during good behavior. The Judges of the Federal Courts can only be removed by impeachment and conviction by the Senate.

If a Judge has attained the age of seventy-five years and has served two consecutive years he may retire on full pay.

What salary do the Judges of the Supreme Court receive?

$10,500 for the Chief Justice and the Associate Judges $10,000, each, per year.

What are the powers of the Supreme Court?

See Constitution.

When does the Supreme Court meet?

At Washington in the Capitol in a chamber formerly occupied by the Senate. The session convenes the second Monday in October and continues until July of every year. The justices all wear black gowns and are the only public officers who use any official dress.

How many constitute a quorum to render a court decision?

Six.

In any case given to the Supreme Court of the United States, is the decision final?

Yes. Every case is discussed by the

whole body twice, once to get the opinion of the majority and then to take final action.

How many Circuit Courts have we?

Nine. Each presiding Judge is assisted by special circuit judges. These courts are held annually. We have now 72 District Courts, 9 Circuit Courts, 9 Appellate Courts the Court of the District of Columbia, Territorial Courts, the Court of Claims, and Consular Courts.

How are the District Courts, Circuit Courts and Courts of Appeals regulated?

By Congress. These Courts are established to relieve the Supreme Court.

What states are classed together in the nine circuit courts?

The first Judicial Circuit: the districts of Maine, New Hampshire, Massachusetts, Rhode Island; Justice Grey.

The second Judicial Circuit: the districts of Vermont, New York, Connecticut; Justice Peckham.

The third Judicial Circuit: the districts of New Jersey, Pennsylvania, Delaware: Justice Shiras.

The fourth Judicial Circuit: the districts of Maryland, Virginia, West Virginia, North Carolina, South Carolina; Chief Justice Fuller.

The fifth Judicial Circuit: The districts of Georgia, Florida, Alabama, Mississippi, Louisiana, Texas; Justice White.

The sixth Judicial Circuit: The districts of Ohio, Michigan, Kentucky, Tennessee; Justice Brown.

The seventh Judicial Circuit: The districts of Indiana, Illinois, Wisconsin; Justice Harlan.

The eighth Judicial Circuit: The districts of Minnesota, North Dakota, South Dakota, Wyoming, Iowa, Missouri, Kansas, Nebraska, Colorado; Justice Brewer.

The ninth Judicial Circuit: The districts of California, Montana, Washington Oregon, Nevada; Justice McKenna.

The Circuit Courts sit in the several districts of each circuit, successively and the law requires that each Justice of the Supreme Court shall sit in each district of his circuit at least once in every two years.

Are there other circuit Judges appointed?

Yes, two or more for each circuit.

At what salary?

$6,000, each.

Who, by virtue of his office, is presiding Judge of th Circuit Court?

One of the Justices of the Supreme Court.

The Circuit Court may be held by the Circuit Judge alone, or by the Supreme Court Circuit Judge alone, or by both together, or by either sitting alone with the District Judge of the District Court.

What are the District Courts?

They are the third and lowest of the Federal Tribunals.

How many Judicial Districts have we?

Seventy-two. Each state is entitled to at least one district.

How many District Judges are there?

Sixty-three. Some of the Judges must preside over two districts.

Each district also has its District Attorney.

What are the duties of a District Attorney?

To prosecute offenders against Federal laws and to conduct civil cases in which the government is either defendant or plaintiff.

The District Attorney is the United States law officer for that District.

The Court of Claims meets in Washington and decides what claims against the United States should be paid.

What salary do the Judges of the Court of Claims receive?

$4,500 a year each.

What salary do the District Judges receive?

$5,000, each.

How are the United States commissioners appointed.

By the Circuit Judges.

Each of the seventy-two districts have a District Marshal and a District Attorney.

How are these appointed?

By the President.

What power has the United States Marshal?

He is the executive officer of the Circuit and District Courts and stands in a similar relation to these that a sheriff does to a county.

When was the Circuit Court of Appeals established?

In 1891.

What are Consular Courts?

They are courts in some cases held by American Consuls in foreign countries. Usually these cases are troubles arising in commercial transactions and are often decided by this Court.

CIVIL SERVICE.

What do we mean by civil service?

That all efficient appointed officers should be retained in service, regardless of politics, during good behavior.

What does our Civil Service include?

All government employes except military and naval officers. It is generally applied to appointed officers and employes in the executive branch of the government and not to the Legislature or Judiciary departments.

Who was the first President to depart from the principles of early Civil Service?

Jefferson, when the "Spoil System" was introduced. The evil of it continued until 1865 when a bill was introduced to reform the Civil Service. In 1871 an act was passed giving the President authority to make rules for admission into the civil service.

What was then done?

A Civil Service commission was appointed with George William Curtis at its head.

What were its duties?

To introduce tests of fitness of applicants.

How long did this continue?

Until 1873, when Congress discontinued the appropriation for this commission.

What bill pertaining to Civil Service reform passed in 1883?

The "Pendleton Act," introduced by Senator Pendleton of Ohio.

What did this act provide?

It provided for a Civil Service commission of three representing both parties, which should provide competitive examinations for entrance into such classes of the Civil Service as the President designates.

Do all applicants for government positions in all the departments have to be examined?

Yes, except as stated above, and if they pass a written examination, they are listed and from this list of persons thus qualified the appointments are made.

What important departments come under Civil Service?

The department service. The postoffice service, The Government Printing Service and Internal Revenue Service.

Can a person in the Civil Service become a member of Congress at the same time.

No.

THE SIGNAL SERVICE.—What are the uses of the Signal Service?

This service is based on the Science of

Meteorology and those engaged in it are largely occupied with the study of weather changes, and the laws of storms, their origin and progress.

When was the Signal Service instituted?

At the beginning of the Civil War, and was first used solely for military purposes.

How is it still conducted?

By the war department. It now estimates the weather probabilities based on scientific observations, and daily reports are published all over the country.

DISTRICT OF COLUMBIA.

How is the District of Columbia governed?

Congress has exclusive control of the District. The Civil Government of the District is vested in three Commissioners, two of whom are appointed by the President with the consent of the Senate for three years, the third is an officer of the Army belonging to the Engineer's Corps, detailed by the President for this service. The duties of these Commissioners are the same as those usually performed by the Mayors and boards of Aldermen.

How are the expenses met?

The expenses of the District Government are equally divided between the U.

S. Congress and the property owners of the District.

Can the people of the District vote?

No. Not in the District.

To what states did the District of Columbia formerly belong?

Maryland and Virginia.

How large was the original District?

One hundred square miles.

How large is it now?

Less than seventy.

When did Congress move to Washington?

In 1800.

Has the District, at any time, been represented in Congress?

Yes by a delegate.

When did the District have a Territorial form of Government?

In 1871 the President and Senate appointed a Governor and a council, and the people elected a house of delegates and a delegate to Congress.

Did this prove a success?

No; it was abolishd in 1874.

TERRITORIES.

Have all the states in the Union once been territories?

All except the thirteen original states.

How many classes of territories have we now?

Two, organized and unorganized.

What is the form of government in an organized territory?

An organized territory has a Governor, Judges, Secretary of Territory and Attorney. All appointed by the President and confirmed by the Senate.

For how long are they appointed?

For a term of four years.

How are they paid?

From the National Treasury.

Of what does the government of a territory consist?

Of legislative, executive and judical branches.

How is the legislative divided?

Into two houses, called the Council and house of Representatives.

How are the members of the legislature elected?

By the qualified electors in the districts of the territory.

Can the territories make their own laws?

Laws passing their legislature are subject to the approval of Congress.

How is an organized territory represented in Congress?

A territory having 5,000 male inhabitants is entitled to a delegate to Congress.

What are the privileges of a delegate?

He can debate motions but cannot vote. He can be appointed on committees.

How is he elected?

The territorial delegate is elected by the vote within the territory.

Do territories elect electors and have an electoral college to vote for President?

No, they have nothing to do with electing the President or Vice President.

How are the territories divided?

Into three judicial districts. Each territory has a Supreme Court and three district courts;—also, there are Justices' Courts.

How many organized territories have we now? (1897)

Three. Oklahoma, Arizona and New Mexico.

How many delegates in Congress?

Three.

How can a territory become a state?

The first act of the territory is to petition Congress through their delegate for admission into the Union.

What is done with the petition?

Congress refers it to the committee on

territories. The committee presents a bill which if passed defines the boundaries and decides on the name of the state, and, also, gives the territory the power to elect dele· gates to the convention to prepare a con· stitution for the state.

What are the special requirements in this act of Congress?

That the constitution for the new state must be republican in form, and it must be in harmony with the constitution of the United States and Declaration of Indepen· dence.

How are the delegates to this convention elected?

By the voters.

What do they do?

Frame a constitution.

What is then done with this proposed constitution?

It is submited to the electors of the ter· ritory to be voted on.

What is next done?.

If the constitution is adopted by a major· ity of electors, the Governor of the territo· ry sends a copy of the adopted constitu· tion to the President of the United States, and if he finds that it complies with the re· quirements made by Congress he issues a proclamation declaring the territory ad mitted as a state into the Union. The people of the state then elect the officers.

What is an unorganized territory?

An unorganized territory is subject only to the laws of Congress.

What territory belongs to this class?

The Indian Territory.

How is Alaska governed?

Alaska is governed entirely by Congress with a Governor appointed by the President and Senate. Alaska has no legislature.

NATURALIZATION. How many years must a foreigner remain in this country before he can take out naturalization papers and become a citizen?

He must reside in the United States five years, and one year in the State or Territory where he asks for admission to citizenship.

What must he do two years before he is admitted to citizenship?

He must renounce allegiance to any foreign prince or state.

Can foreigners vote at state elections before they take out their naturalization papers?

That is governed by the laws of the states. In more than one third of the states the election franchise is granted foreigners, before they are naturalized, by declaring their intention of becoming American citizens.

If naturalized citizens go abroad are they still protected by the United States?

Yes: the statutes of the United States say that "all naturalized citizens of the United States while in foreign countries are entitled to and shall receive from this Government the same protection of person and property which is accorded to native-born citizens."

LIBRARY OF CONGRESS.

Where is the largest Library Building in the world?

The Library of Congress at Washington, which has a capacity of five million volumes. This is considered the most gorgeous building in America.

When was the Library of Congress established?

By an act of Congress in 1800.

When was it destroyed?

When the British burned the Capitol in 1814. It was reestablished by Congress in the same year in the central capitol building.

When was it again partially destroyed by fire?

In 1851.

What act was passed in 1824?

An act to appropriate five thousand dollars annually for the purchase of library books.

What did the present Library cost? $5,700,000.

OUR FLAG.

Flag of the free hearts hope and home!
By angel hands to valor given;
Thy stars have lit the welkin dome,
And all thy hues were born in heaven.
Forever float that standard sheet
Where breathes the foe but falls before us,
With freedom's soil beneath our feet
And freedom's banner streaming o'er us?

   —Joseph Rodman Drake.

When was our American Flag adopted by the Continental Congress?

June 14th, 1777.

What decree was issued in this Congress?

"That the flag of the United States be thirteen stripes, alternate red and white; that the union be thirteen stars, white on a blue field, representing a new constellation."

During the early days of the Revolution what flag was used?

Various designs were made and used.

The flag used by the Americans at the battle of Bunker Hill was called the "New England Flag." This was a blue ground with the red cross of St. George in the corner and in the upper staff corner a green pine tree. Different flags were designed and used until 1775, when Congress appointed a committee to make a design for a Union flag.

Who was on this Committee?

Dr. Franklin, who suggested they visit General Washington to get his opinion on a design.

A design was finally submitted to the committee, the committee submitted it to Mrs. Betsey Ross, who was a seamstress. She made suggestions for the present flag and made the first American flag with stars and stripes.

What act was passed April 1818 pertaining to the flag?

That the number of stripes be limited to thirteen and the number of stars increase with the number of states; that is, a new star was to be added on the fourth of July next succeeding the admission of any new state.

Who is supposed to have first unfurled the national flag?

Paul Jones on the Ranger, (a naval vessel), on the day Congress passed the resolution to adopt it as the national flag.

Is the flag always displayed on the Capitol Building while Congress is in session? Yes.

LIBERTY BELL.

What is the Liberty Bell?

It is the Bell that announced the Declaration of Independence in 1776.

Where was this bell cast?

Originally in London in 1752 and recast in Philadelphia in 1753, and hung in the Pennsylvania State House, afterwards known as Independence Hall.

What is inscribed on the Bell?

"Proclaim Liberty throughout all the Land, unto all the Inhabitants thereof."

When was it cracked?

July 8th, 1835 while being tolled in memory of Chief Justice Marshall.

What became of this Bell?

It is still kept in Independence Hall in Philadelphia.

A new bell was made to take the place of the old one in 1828.

When was another bell made and called the "New Liberty Bell?"

In 1892. It was made from various pieces and kinds of money and metal presented by the people of the U. S. for the purpose. It was exhibited and dedicated at the World's Fair in 1893.

THE GREAT SEAL OF THE UNITED STATES.

When was the U. S. Seal adopted?

In 1782—June 20th.

Who designed the seal?

On July 4th, 1776 Congress appointed Benjamin Franklin, John Adams and Thomas Jefferson a committee to prepare a device for the seal. After several designs were submitted the present one was adopted.

What does the seal represent?

It represents a spread eagle, the emblem of strength, wearing on its breast an escutcheon of thirteen stripes, alternate red and white like the national flag. In its right talon the eagle holds 'an olive branch, the emblem of peace, and in its left talon are thirteen arrows representing the thirteen states. In its beak is a scroll with the motto "E Pluribus Unum," meaning "many in one,"—many states, one nation. Over the head is a golden light breaking through a cloud and surrounding thirteen stars, forming a constellation on a blue ground. On the reverse is an unfinished pyramid, representing the unfinished republic, also its strength and duration. Above the pyramid is an eye, denoting the all-seeing eye of Providence, and over this eye are the words "Annuit Coeptis"—"God favors the undertaking." On the base of the pyramid is the Roman date of 1776, and below the pyramid are the words, "Novus ordo sectorum"—A new order of the age." The latter was for a pendant seal, not now used. The recumbent seal, the obverse above described, being always used.

LIBERTY ENLIGHTENING THE WORLD.

Where is the Statue of "Liberty Enlightening the World" placed?

In the Harbor of the City of New York?

When did we get it?

It was given to the people of the United States by the people of France in 1876.

This Statue is typical of the friendship of two powerful nations.

DUTY, TAX, SINGLE TAX, ETC.

What is tax?

Tax is a charge made by the Government against the people or property for the support of the Government.

What is duty?

Duty is a charge laid on articles taken out of or brought into a country.

What is Import Duty?

A tax levied on goods brought into a country.

What is an Excise Tax?

A tax levied on manufactured articles within a country.

A schedule of duties placed by the Government on goods either exported or imported. Tariffs are defined as Tariff for revenue and Tariff for protection. Our tariff is a duty charged for placing on the American market, goods of foreign manufacture.

What is a protective tariff?

A tariff on articles which are imported from abroad and which are also produced in this country, that the American manufacturer with higher rates of wages and interest to pay, than his foreign competitor, may, nevertheless compete with him in the American market.

What is meant by tariff for revenue only?

It means a tariff that provides revenue for the Government without intentionally giving protection to domestic industries.

What is Free Trade?

Free Trade is that theory whose purpose is to secure by import duties, money to pay government expenses by the least possible interference of exchange. In such a case the duties are mainly laid on articles not produced in this country, and which therefore cannot materially effect natural prices for most articles.

What is an Income Tax?

A tax imposed on all incomes over a certain sum per annum.

What is revenue?

It is the annual income of a country derived from taxation, customs, (excise or other sources, and appropriated to the payment of the national expense. The revenue of the United States is derived from the Customs, Internal Revenue, Direct Tax, Public Lands and other sources.

What are Customs?

Duties coming from taxes on importations.

What is Internal Revenue?

Revenue coming from taxes on spirits, tobacco, and fermented liquors.

What is Direct Tax?

Direct Tax is tax upon the person or estate of a citizen, such as houses, lands, moneys, etc.

SINGLE TAX FROM A SINGLE TAXER'S STANDPOINT.

What is The Single Tax?

It is a moral and fiscal reform promulgated by Henry George.

What is its fundamental principle?

The self evident truth that all men are

created equal, and are endowed by their creator with certain inalienable rights.

What are these rights?

The equal right to the use and enjoyment of what God has created and what is gained by the general growth and improvement of the community of which they are a part.

How is it proposed to enforce these rights?

No one should be permitted to hold natural opportunities without a fair return to all for any special privilege thus accorded him, and that value which the growth and improvement of the community attaches to land should be taken for the use of the community; that each is entitled to all his labor produces; therefore no tax should be levied on the products of labor.

How should taxes be levied?

By raising all public revenues for National, State, County and Municipal purposes by a single tax upon land values, irrespective of improvements, and all the obligations of all forms of direct and indirect taxation.

How should the Single Tax be instituted?

By the simple and easy way of abolishing, one after another, all other taxes now levied and commensurately increasing the tax on land values, until we draw upon that one source for all expenses of government.

How would this affect the ownership of land?

It would not disturb existing titles, but, would make the holding of land unprofitable to the mere owner, and profitable only to the user. Thus making speculation in land impossible.

What is the position of Single Taxers on monopolies, such as telegraph lines, railroads, water and gas supplies, etc?

Such business as requires a grant from the people for its operation becomes a proper social function which should be controlled and managed by and for the whole people concerned through their proper government,—local, state or national,—as may be.

How would the Single Tax affect agricultural districts?

It would take the weight of taxation off the agricultural districts where land has little or no value irrespective of improvements and put it on towns and cities where bare land rises to a value of millions of dollars per acre.

For further information read the works of Henry George and "National Taxation," by Thomas G. Shearman.

What is Reciprocity?

It is free interchange or equality of commercial privileges between the subjects of different governments, in each other's ports, with respect to shipping and trading of merchandise to the extent established by treaty.

COPYRIGHTS.   What is a copyright?

The exclusive right to print and dispose of copies of an intellectual production.

The authors of books, maps, engravings, pictures, etc., may obtain the exclusive right to print and sell the same for a period of twenty-eight years. The copyright may be renewed for fourteen years longer.

How may a copyright be obtained?

Two copies must be deposited with the Librarian of Congress at Washington, D.C., and the legal fee of fifty cents for recording.. The certificate is also fifty cents.

Can copyrights be granted on Trade marks?

No; but if protection for names and labels is desired they must be registered at the Patent Office with a fee of six dollars for labels and twenty-five dollars for trade marks.

What special act was passed in Congress in 1891?

Granting the privilege of copyright to foreigners of nations whose governments gave American citizens the same privilege.

PATENTS. What do we mean by patents?

Giving the inventor the exclusive right of making and selling his inventions.

Where are they secured?

Applications of patents are made to the commissioner of Patents, at Washington, D. C.

For how long do they run?

For seventeen years, they may then be renewed by an improvement in the invention.

MONEY.

What is money?

Any thing that serves as a common medium of exchange and measure of value.

Who alone has authority to coin money?

Congress.

What is currency?

Any medium of exchange that is current, whether it be coin, paper or commodities. It is however commonly applied in this country to paper money.

How many kinds of paper money in this country?

Four: Treasury Notes, National Bank Notes, Gold Certificates and Silver Certificates.

What are Treasury Notes?

United States bills issued on the credit of the Government. These notes are legal tender at their face value for all debts public and private, except duties on imports and interest on the public debt.

What are National Bank Notes?

They are notes issued by the National Banks and guaranteed by the Government, the banks depositing United States bonds as security.

These notes are legal tender in payment of taxes and dues to the government and for all dues from the United States to the individual, except, they are not legal tender for import duties, interest on the Public Debt or between individuals.

What are Gold and Silver Certificates?

They are notes issued by the Government against deposits of gold and silver coin or bullion and may be exchanged for such on demand.

What are the coins?

Gold, Silver, Nickel, and Copper.

What is a legal tender, in payment of all debts public and private under all circumstances and conditions?

Gold coin.

What money was used previous to the Revolutionary War?

Mostly foreign. Principally, English coins and Spanish mill dollars; also, some paper money issued by the assemblies of the different colonies, and based on the credit of the colony issuing.

When were our mints for coining established?

In 1792 by act of Congress. Many ex-periments were made in coinage but nothing actually established until 1794.

Where was the first mint established?

In Philadelphia.

Where are our mints for coining money now located?

At Philadelphia, San Francisco, New Orleans and Carson City.

Where are our Assay offices?

New York; Charlotte, North Carolina; Boise City, Idaho; and Denver, Colorado.

When was silver first coined in the United States?

In 1792. Gold was coined the following year.

What is bimetallism?

It is the name given to a monetary sys-tem in which both gold and silver are on precisely the same footing as regards mint-age and legal tender.

What is monometallism?

The doctrine that only one metal should

be used as a standard of value.

What is meant by the Gold Standard?

It means that gold is made the legal measure of all moneys and values.

What is meant by Free Coinage of Silver?

It means the coinage into money of silver bullion by any one presenting the same at the U. S. mint for that purpose.

What is the present ratio of gold and silver?

16 to 1.

What is meant by coinage of Gold and Silver 16 to 1?

It means that a silver dollar shall contain sixteen times the weight of silver that a gold dollar contains of gold.

When was the first greenback issued?

In 1862.

What is "fiat" money?

Any currency whether paper or metal that is placed in circulation and maintained as legal tender by command of the government.

When was " fiat" money first issued in this country?

Fiat money in small amounts was issued by Pennsylvania and other colonies long before the Revolutionary War. This money was suppressed by the English Crown.

During the Revolutionary War the continental Congress issued fiat money of different denominations, but the Congress having no power to levy taxes and being obliged to furnish resources, issued large amounts which the colonial government could not redeem and they became worthless in 1780. The English government counterfeited them by the milloins. Without this fiat money the Continental army would have failed and Independence not have been achieved.

What can be done with Greenbacks that are burned?

The charred and blackened remains are sent to the Treasury for replacement. The identification of these bills so burned is in the hands of an expert woman in the Comptroller's office.

What can be done with mutilated paper money?

When the paper money becomes dirty and torn and it is presented to the United States Treasury, new notes may be exchanged for them.

What becomes of the old money?

Every working day one million dollars are destroyed after a proper record has been made of the old bills. They are placed in large chests and carried to the basement of the Treasury building and at 2 p. m. each day three officials meet, one representing the Secretary of the Treasury, one the Treasurer of the United States, and the third the Comptroller of Currency. Each bank whose money is to be destroyed is required to have a representative present to see that the money is properly disposed of. These old bills are then put in a hopper with a large revolving cylinder containing steam and chemicals, which converts the paper into a soft pulp which, afterwards, is sold.

What are Government Bonds?

They are bonds issued by the Government as evidence of indebtedness for money it has borrowed or for obligations it has assumed.

BANKS.

What is a bank?

An institution for negotiating credits, for discounting notes, for issue of paper money and a place for deposit of valuables.

What is banking?

Trading in and with money such as buying, selling, exchanging and dealing in credit.

What are the officers of a bank called?
Bankers.

What is the oldest bank on record?
The Bank of Venice established 1171.

What bank is the most important one in the world?

The Bank of England.

When was it established?

It was proposed by William Paterson. A bill was passed by the Government, and a charter granted April, 1694, for eleven years.

What advantage has an American married woman over an English woman as pertaining to banking?

In England a married woman cannot open a bank account unless she has in writing the formal consent of her husband. Neither can a woman who has opened an account with an English bank, while she was a single person, withdraw that money after she is married, unless, she has the approval of her husband.   In America she has practically the same rights and privileges, in law, as an unmarried woman.

When were banks first established in the United States?

The first bank chartered in the United States was the Bank of North America in 1781.   This bank had a ten year charter and was located in Philadelphia.

Who was the founder of this bank?

Robert Morris.

When was the first United States bank chartered?

In 1790 Alexander Hamilton, then Secretary of the Treasury, recommended in his report the establishing of the Bank of the U. S.. His plan was adopted by Congress and a charter granted in 1791 with a capital of $10,000,000. This bank issued no bills under ten dollars.

Who may conduct banks?

Capitalists may unite under the laws of the United States and form a National Banking association; or a number under a state law and organize a state bank; or one person or company may conduct an individual or private bank.

What is a private bank?

A private bank is one conducted by an individual, or company, without a charter, and hence under less restriction than a state or national bank.

If banks are organized under state laws what are they required to do?

They are bound by the law and subject to inspection. They must also pay a tax of ten per cent on the amount of money used in their business, and, if they issue promises to pay, a coin reserve must be kept to pay them.

When were national banks established?

They were authorized in 1863 and established in 1864.

What is meant by a national bank?

A national bank is not owned or conducted by the Government, but it authorizes its creation and prescribes its mode of doing business. All national banks come under the same law in every state, are subject to the same inspection, and use the same blanks in making returns to the Treasury department at Washington.

How are national banks organized?

Under the National Law, a banking association may be formed by five or more persons, who must specify in their articles of association the general object of thus uniting. They must make out their "organization certificate."

1st.   The name of the organization.

2nd.   Place of business.

3rd.   The amount of its stock and the number of shares into which it is divided.

4th.   The names and residences of the share holders and the number of shares held by each.

5th.   A declaration that the certificate is made to enable them to avail themselves of the advantage of this title.

What is done with these organization certificates?

They must be signed by the persons uniting to form the association and be acknowledged before a judge of some court of record or notary public and together with the acknowledgement by the seal of said court, must be sent to the Comptroller of Curren cy to be filed and preserved in his office.

What is the capital stock required?

No association can be organized with a less capital than one hundred thousand dollars under this title, except, that banks with a capital of not less than fifty thousand dollars, may, with the approval of the treasury, be organized in any place where the population does not exceed six thousand inhabitants. No association can be organized in a city, the population of which exceeds fifty thousand persons, with less than two hundred thousand dollars.

If a national bank is organized in a small place with capital stock of fifty thousand dollars can it continue with that stock if the town increases to more than six thousand people?

Yes.

What are the corporate powers of a national bank association?

After incorporation it has power:

First. To adopt and use a corporate seal.

Second. To do business for the period of twenty years from its organization unless it is sooner dissolved according to the provisions of its Articles of Association, or by the act of its shareholders owning two-thirds of its stock, or unless its franchise becomes forfeited by some violation of law.

Third. To make contracts.

Fourth. To sue and be sued.

Fifth. To elect or appoint a board of directors; and this board in turn appoints the President, Vice-President, Cashier and other officers.

Sixth. To prescribe, by its board of directors, "by-laws" not inconsistent with law, regulate the manner in which its stock shall be transferred, etc.

Seventh. To exercise by its board of directors or duly authorized agents, subject to law, all such incidental powers as are necessary to carry on the banking business.

How is the capital stock divided?

The capital stock, of each association, is divided into shares of one hundred dollars each and it is to be deemed as personal property.

Can these shares be transferred?

Yes;by vote of the association in such a manner as may be prescribed in the by-laws of the organization. Each person becoming a shareholder by such transfers will, in proportion to his shares, succeed to all rights and liberties of the prior holder of such shares.

How many directors must each National

Banking Association have?

They must have not less than five directors, who are elected by the share holders at a meeting held any time before the association is authorized by the Comptroller of currency to commence business. The directors hold office for one year and until their successors are elected and qualified. From the board of directors one is chosen its president. Each director is entitled to one vote for each share of stock held by him. Shareholders may vote by proxies, duly authorized in writing. No shareholder whose liability is passed and unpaid is allowed to vote. Each director is required to take an oath of office, and this is filed with the comptroller of currency.

Must directors be citizens of the United States?

Every director must, during his whole term of service, be a citizen of the United States, and at least three-fourths of the directors must have resided in the state or territory or district, in which the association is located, for at least one year immediately preceding the election, and must reside therein during their continuance in office.

How many shares must each director own?

Each and every director must own in his

own right at least ten shares of capital
stock of the association in which he is a director. Any director who has ceased to
be owner of ten shares of stock, or who becomes in any other manner disqualified,
must thereby vacate his place.

When must the capital stock be paid in?

At least fifty per centum of the capital
stock of every association must be paid in
before it can be authorized to commence
business; and the remainder of the capital
must be paid in installments of at least ten
per centum, each, on the whole amount of
the capital, as frequently as one install-
ment at the end of each succeeding month
from the time it shall be authorized by the
comptroller of the currency to commence
business, and the payment of each install-
ment must be certified to the comptroller
under oath by the president or cashier of
the organization.

After all the provisions required by law
have been complied with, what does the
comptroller do?

He grants the association a certificate
under his hand and official seal, authoriz-
ing them to commence business.

What is then done by the association?

They must have their certificate published in newspapers printed in the city or
county where the association is located,

for at least sixty days next after the issuing thereof. They are then ready to begin business.

Where do the profits of bankers come from?

From the interest on the government bonds deposited by the association with the United States Treasurer, and from discounts in negtiating loans, etc. Also, the excess of the interest he receives from those indebted to him over the interest he allows to those who have deposited money or paper with him.

How may money be paid out?

By checks or drafts.

What are bank notes?

Bank notes are obligations issued by a bank to pay a certain specified sum to the bearer on demand.

Are national bank notes taken everywhere in the United States?

Yes; because they are protected by the government bond deposited with the Treasurer of the United States.

How is the clerical work done in banks?

By cashiers, bookkeepers and tellers.

CLEARING HOUSE.

What is a clearing house?

An establishment where the process of clearing or settling accounts is carried on.

When was the first clearing house for bankers established?

It was established in London in 1775. It was used as a place where clerks of banks of that city would meet daily to exchange with one another the checks drawn upon, and bills payable at their respective houses.

When was the first bank clearing house established in theUnited States?

1853, in New York City.

What becomes of a check? Follow a check from the time you pay a bill with it until it is returned to you.

The person receiving it may in turn pay it over to some one else, they, themselves, endorsing it on the back; or it may be by them turned over to the bank to be deposited to his account. If it is a check on the same bank as deposited it is simply held there until your bank book is balanced, when it is returned to you, together with other checks you have issued.

If it is presented to the bank and cashed and the check belongs to some other bank, what becomes of it?

Every check is stamped with the number of the bank which is sending it to the clearing house. At a certain hour all the checks are taken by a clerk and these checks are exchanged and balances made.

These checks are taken back to their respective banks and finally returned to the depositor.

DIRECT LEGISLATION.

Where is the germ of a perfect government to be found?

In the authority of the people.

What is claimed in regard to the ballot in the United States by those who believe in direct legislation?

That it has ceased to be an expression of the will of the people.

How is it claimed the will of the people can be restored?

By the establishment of a pure democracy.

What is meant by direct legislation?

A pure democracy. It is for the people to vote for laws instead of voting for representatives and delegate to them the full power of making the laws.

What is the referendum?

It is the right of the people to pass upon all laws, and by a majority vote accept or reject them.

What is the initiative.

It is the right of a citizen, or citizens, under certain necessary restrictions, to initiate any needed legislation.

What is the imperative mandate?

It is the right of the people to remove any public officer, without regard for the length of time for which he may have been elected, who has proved unfaithful.

What is claimed as to present methods of legislation?

That they are cumbrous, inefficient and easily abused.

What is the method proposed?

More direct legislation, this being guaranteed by the spirit and words of the Declaration of Independence. More definitely this method is defined as the Referendum, The Initiative, and The Imperative Mandate.

What about the results?

Legislative bodies would become simply committees of the people to attend routine business and consider measures. Which must be submitted to the people before final enactment into law. No legislation, except such as the majority of the people approve can become law. The standard of citizenship would be raised and the corrupt lobby would disappear from the halls of legislation. When a question is once settled right it cannot be undone by a change of legislators, or of a political party for party purposes. Promises made the people by a successful candidate would have to be fulfilled and all questions would be discussed on their merits.

When would the Initiative be used?

Only when the representatives (the com-
mitees) of the people failed to see or do
their duty.

Would a change in the method of voting
take place?

Not necessarily. But some think it
would be great economy for the Postoffice
department, with a small increase of the
force, to collect the vote of the people. The
secret ballot and strict registration laws
would no longer be required. The expense
of making laws would be reduced and time
for consideration of all measures would be
given.

How would the Initiative be used?

A convention of about 300 voters would
be held and the proposed law or governmental policy formulated and signed by at
least five percent of the voters in the terri-
troy represented. The document would
then be deposited with the clerk of city or
county, who transmits a copy to the President. It is then caused to be printed and
copies sent to every postoffice, half of the
expense to be borne by the Initiative Convention and half by the government. This
would prevent voters resorting to the Initiative unless urgent necessity arose.
When the Post Master receives the docu-

ment he displays it on a bulletin and every voter showing his electoral card will be allowed to record his vote in a book kept for that purpose at the Postoffice. The Post Master transmits the votes to the county clerk, the clerk to the governor and the governor to the Speaker of the House. If the total from all the states reaches the percent of signers the House will frame a measure in accordance with the petition and "submit it to the people at the annual referendary ballot."

How would the Referendum be conducted?

Congress would fix a day for the annual referendary vote; a day four or six months after the adjournment of Congress. All bills and questions would be properly printed for distribution to the Postoffices. If the people desire they can vote on them. If they should be satisfied with them they can approve and if dissatisfied they can veto. It is claimed the United States Senate might be abolished and legislatures would be unnecessary, as a committee would be sufficient. Great economy is promised in every department of government and the saving of millions of dollars.

SWITZERLAND as an example of the Initiative and Referendum.

What is one of the oldest republics of the world?

Switzerland.

How long has it been a republic?

For over five hundred years.

Of what was it composed?

Of independent cantons, each of which had its laws, a simple republic within itself, and, except in times of war, they had but little communication between them. There was no strong central government. In more recent years great changes have taken place. Revolutions sprung up in the cantons, a new general constitution was adopted in 1848 modeled somewhat after that of the United States. All the monarchies protested against the Swiss constitution and predicted dire failure.. The constitution was again amended in 1874, so as to give strength of union and yet maintain more direct legislation on the part of the people. It is the purest democracy in the world among civilized nations.

How many cantons in the Swiss Republic?

Twenty-two.

What is the total population?

3,000,000.

How many languages are spoken in the parliament at Bern?

Three, German, French and Italian. A motion made in German is quickly repeated in French and Italian before discussion or a vote is taken. Most of the Swiss Parliamentarians understand the three languages, and many of them English. A trained statesman who can serve the people well is apt to be retained at his post.

To whom are the laws submitted for approval after adoption in the Diet?

To the people.

Who holds the final veto power?

The people.

How do the people of Switzerland use the intitiative?

If thirty thousand citizens, or eight cantons, demand it by petition any act of their parliament must be submitted to a vote of the whole people.

How is the president elected?

By Parliament.

How is the Governing Council elected?

This Council corresponds to our President's Cabinet and is composed of seven men selected by Parliament from among its own members. A "political accident" could not become a president or a member of the Council.

What salary does the President and members of Parliament receive?

The President receives $2,000.00 and the members $1,000.00.

For how long is the President elected?

For one year.

Who appoints the members of the Su-reme Court?

Parliament.

What relation to Parliament does the President and Council sustain?

They are members of one branch or the other of Parliament.

How are the members of Parliament elected?

The lower house is chosen, by the peo-ple, and the constitution provides that the Senators may be chosen by the people or by the legislatures.

For how long are they chosen?

They are chosen for three years.

How often does Parliament meet?

Yearly or it may meet oftener if one-fourth of the members of the upper house command it.

There are no secret sessions in this Par-liament.

What is the power of the people in leg-islation?

They may reject any or all bills adopted by Parliament.

Who owns the Railroads and telegraph lines in Switzerland?

The government.

What is a peculiar characteristic of this law-making?

Important laws are often several years in process of enactment, but when made the laws must be obeyed. The Statute Books are not burdened with many useless or neglected laws.

What advantage is claimed for the Referendum and veto power in the hands of the people?

A copy of the law to be voted on is placed in the hands of each voter and he must examine and pass upon it. No voter can plead ignorance of the law.

Switzerland is the first country to practice direct legislation.

POLITICAL SAYINGS.

What great man said, "I'd rather be right than President of the United States?"

Henry Clay.

Under what circumstances?

He had introduced a bill in Congress in 1833 to reduce the then existing duties in order to favor the Agricultural States. Some of the Southern States opposed this measure, and when told he would lose his chances for the Presidency he made the above statement.

Who said, "I was born an American, I live an American, I shall die an American?"

Daniel Webster, in a speech delivered July 17, 1850.

Who said "I am not a Virginian, I am an American?"

Patrick Henry, in the First Continental Congress.

What General said "I propose to fight it out on this line if it takes all summer?"

General Grant to the Secretary of War.

What President said "To be prepared for war, is one of the most effectual means of preserving peace?"

George Washington.

What President in his second inaugural

address said, "With malice toward none with charity for all?"

Abraham Lincoln.

Who was commonly known and called the "Father of the Constitution?"

James Madison.

Why was he called that?

Because he was the author of the resolution that led to the invitation for the Convention of 1787 issued by the Virginia Legislature.

Where do we find these words,"First in war, first in peace, and first in the hearts of his countrymen?"

In a resolution passed in the House of Representatives on the death of George Washington.

What striking utterance did Benjamin Franklin make after the passage of the Stamp Act?

He said: "The Americans must light the lamps of Industry and Economy."

In giving instructions to our ministers abroad as to what our foreign policy should be who said, "Ask nothing but what is right, submit to nothing wrong?"

Andrew Jackson.

Who said, "We must all hang together or we shall all hang separately?"

Benjamin Franklin when signing the Declaration of Independence.

Who was called the "Expounder of the Constitution?"

Daniel Webster.

Who said "Government of the people, by the people, and for the people shall not perish from the Earth?"

Abraham Lincoln in his famous Gettysburg address.

What President said "A pound of pluck is worth a ton of luck?"

James A. Garfield.

Who was called the "Cincinnatus of the West?"

George Washington.

What great American orator said, "Give me liberty or give me death?"

Patrick Henry in a speech before the Virginia Convention in 1775 in favor of a resolution "That the Colony be immediately put in a state of defense." In the closing of his remarks he said, "Is life so dear, or peace so sweet as to be purchased at the price of chains and slavery? Forbid it, Almighty God! I know not what course others may take, but as for me, give me liberty or give me death."

What was said by James A. Garfield the morning after Lincoln was assassinated?

"God reigns and the Government at Washington still lives."

On what occassion did he say it?

In a brief speech, when a crowd were about to attack a newspaper which had violently opposed Lincoln. Garfield appeared in the midst and in a speech before the crowd said: "Fellow Citizens! Clouds and darkness are round about Him. His pavilion is dark waters and thick clouds of skies. Justice and judgment are the establishment of His throne. Mercy and truth shall go before His face. Fellow citizens! God reigns, and the government at Washington still lives."

Who was styled "Old Public Functionary?"

James Buchanan.

Who said of Alexander Hamilton that "He smote the rock of the national resources and abundant streams of revenue gushed forth?"

Daniel Webster.

Whose cabinet was known as the "Kitchen Cabinet?"

Andrew Jackson's.

Who said "Millions for defense, but not a cent for tribute?"

Charles C. Pinckney.

Who received the famous "X Y Z dispatches?

John Adams.

At the Continental Congress who said, "I am not worth purchasing, but such as I am, the King of Great Britain is not rich enough to do it?"

Joseph Reed, a member of the Congress, when offered a large sum of money to use his influence to restore the colonies to Great Britain.

Who was known as "the Master of Elegance?"

Edward Everett.

Who was the author of the expression "They see nothing wrong in the rule that to the victors belong the spoils?"

William L. Marcy in 1832, in speaking of the removal from office of those who had been appointed under the previous administrations.

What president announced in his last annual message "The country was without a national bank and without a permanent national debt?"

Martin Van Buren.

He was president from 1837 to 1841.

Who said "He touched the dead corpse of public credit and it sprung upon its feet?"

Daniel Webster of Alexander Hamilton.

Whence came the motto "Americans must rule America?"

From the "Know Nothings."

Whom did Bancroft call the "wisest civilian of them all?"

James Madison.

MISCELLANEOUS QUESTIONS.

What college first admitted women?

Oberlin, at Oberlin, Ohio.

Who was the first woman to be elected president of a college in America?

Francis E. Willard, who was made president of the Evanston College for women in Feb. 1871.

When were envelopes first used?

1839.

How long have postage stamps been used?

In England since 1840. In the United States since 1847.

When was printing introduced in America?

In 1539, in the City of Mexico, and in Cambridge, Mass., in 1639. It was first known in China in the sixth century.

When was the first public school established in the United States?

In 1635, in Boston.

Where did our present public system originate?

In New England, 1649, by law of the colony.

What was the first territory admitted as a state with woman's suffrage at the time of its admission?

Wyoming.

How long have women voted in Wyoming?

Since 1869.

What state first elected women representatives to its state legislature?

Colorado, in 1894.

What state elected the first woman state senator?

Utah, 1896.

Mrs. Martha Hughes Cannon.

What state elected the first woman presidential elector?

Wyoming, 1896.

Who was it?

Mrs. Sarah Malloy.

When did free delivery of mail matter by carriers first take effect?

July first, 1863.

When was the "reply" postal card issued?

In 1892.

Are stamped envelopes, if misdirected, ever redeemable?

Yes, upon application to the postoffice department.

What woman's face has ever adorned United States paper money?

The face of Martha Washington.

What is bullion?

Uncoined gold and silver bars.

What is the Monroe doctrine?

It is the doctrine in American politics of non-intervention of European powers in matters relating to American continents, and is opposed to any extension of territory on the part of such powers upon this continent.

What is meant by the term "dark horse?"

It is the term applied to the successful nominee of a party who was little known at the time of the nomination, or one whose nomination was not generally expected.

To whom was it first applied?

To James K. Polk.

When was the first bank of the United States chartered?

By congress in 1791. It was opened for the transaction of business in Carpenter's Hall, at Philadelphia, in December of the same year.

How may war be declared?

Only by a bill passing both houses of congress and signed by the president. The senate may make a treaty of peace.

How did "Uncle Sam" originate?

The nickname of "Uncle Sam," as applied to the United States government, is said to originate with Samuel Wilson, commonly called "Uncle Sam," a government inspector of beef and pork, at Troy , N. Y., in 1812. A contractor, Elbert Anderson, purchased a quantity of provisions. The barrels came marked "E. A.,"—Anderson's initials—"U. S." (United States.) Wilson's workmen not being familiar with the latter initials, inquired what they meant, and one fellow answered, "I don't know, unless they mean Uncle Sam."

Who is known as the "bewildered con- gressman?"

James E. Cobb of Alabama, who, while delivering an address in congress, having been diverted from the order of his re- marks, said: "Mr. Speaker, where am I at?"

What are the great naval powers of the world?

Great Britian stands pre-eminently first as the most important, France second, Rus- sia third, Italy fourth and the United States fifth.

What is a congressman at large?

One elected by the voters of a whole state, instead of a single district, which is done when the existing apportionment by districts does not provide for all the repre- sentatives to which the state is entitled.

Who is speaker of the house of Lords in England?

The Lord Chancellor.

How is the speaker of the house of commons in England chosen?

By the House, subject to the approval of the crown.

What is the difference between the English and American enacting clause of a bill?

The English enacting clause reads, "Be it enacted by the Queen's most excellent majesty, by and with the consent of the Lords, spiritual and temporal, and the Commons and by the authority of the same. The American enacting clause: "Be it enacted by the Senate and House of Representatives of the United States of America, in Congress assembled."

When was the first recorded Thanksgiving day?

In 1631 in the Massachusetts Bay colony.

Who appointed the first national Thanksgiving day?

President Washington, for November, 1789.

When was the Tammany society of New York organized?

In 1789 by William Mooney, an upholsterer, and named after St. Tammany, a noted Delaware chief, of whom it is said he loved "liberty more than life."

When was "E Pluribus Unum" first used as a motto?

It first appeared on coins in New Jersey in 1786, when copper coins were issued in the state, and was suggested by Franklin, John Adams and Jefferson as a motto of the United States, and as a design for the great seal.

To whom and when was the first diploma granted to a woman?

To Mrs. Elizabeth Blackwell, Geneva, N. Y., in 1849.

When was letter postage reduced to two cents?

In 1883.

When were copyright and patent laws first enacted in this country?

In 1784 in South Carolina. Such a general law passed congress in 1790.

When and where was the first mint established in the English-American colonies?

In Boston, 1652.

What special stamp privilege was granted Washington for life?

That of receiving his letters free of postage, which courtesy has subsequently been granted to every President and Ex-President and their widows.

When was the White House built?

The corner stone was laid in 1792, and first occupied by President Adams in 1800. It was burned by the British in 1814, and restored in 1817.

When was Decoration Day established?

It is claimed to have been established in 1863, while some claim 1862.

What state is called the mother of presidents?

Virginia, and it is also called the mother of states, and it was the first state settled of the thirteen states that formed the union.

Who was the author of the expression "The Almighty Dollar?"

Washington Irving wrote it as a satire on the American love for gain.

Which is the oldest college in America?

Harvard college. It was established in 1638.

Who was known as "Alexander, the Coppersmith?"

Alexander Hamilton, by those who were dissatisfied with the copper cent coined in 1793.

To whom were these words applied, "All quiet along the Potomac?"

To Gen. McClellan, when his army, fully

equipped, remained so long inactive in 1861.

When was "Arbor Day" inaugurated?

In 1865, by the state board of education of Connecticut.

Who were known as "Carpet-baggers?"

The term was applied to the northerners who went south after the war for political purposes without intending to permanently settle.

When did "Copperheads," as an epithet, originate?

It was the name given to northern sympathizers with the south during the civil war.

What is the Mason and Dixon line?

The line which separates Pennsylvania and Maryland. It was practically the line which separated the free from the slave states in the east.

Who was known as the "Mill Boy of the Sluices?"

Henry Clay.

What is known as the "Cradle of Liberty?"

Faneuil Hall, Boston.

What is known as the "dollar of our dads?"

It is a nickname for the silver dollar.

Who was known as the "Noblest Roman of them all?"

Allen G. Thurman.

Who was known as "Old Hickory?"

Andrew Jackson.

Who was commonly called "Old Man Eloquent?"

John Quincy Adams.

To whom was "Old Rough and Ready" applied?

Gen. Zachary Taylor.

Who was called "Old Saddle Bags?"

Joseph McDonald, of Indiana.

When was the first woman's club organized in Germany?

January, 1897, in Berlin.

Who was the first woman novelist?

Frances Burney (Madam D'Arbley.)

What is known as the "Liberty Tree?"

The tree on which Andrew Oliver was hung in effigy in 1765, because he had agreed to become distributer of stamps under the famous stamp act, which passed that year.

When was the first library established in America?

In 1638, at Harvard college—the first public library in New York City in 1700.

What was the last piece of country

bought by the United States from a foreign power?

Alaska; bought from Russia March, 1867,, for $7,200,000 in gold.

When was the first steamboat invented?

In 1807 by Robt. Fulton, and called the "Steamer Clermont."

What is meant by "Plymouth Rock?"

The place where our forefathers first stepped on land in this country.

Where is this place?

At Plymouth, Mass.

When was the first newspaper printed in America?

In 1704, "The Boston News," published at Boston, Mass.

Who wrote the Declaration of Independence?

Thomas Jefferson.

Who were the committee to draft the Declaration of Independence?

Thomas Jefferson, John Adams, Robert Livingston, Benjamin Franklin and Roger Sherman.

What closed the Revolutionary war?

The surrender of Cornwallis at Yorktown, October 19, 1781.

To whom did Cornwallis surrender?

To General Washington.

When was the treaty of peace signed?
September 3d, 1783, at Paris, France.

What state was admitted into the Union
first after our independence?

Vermont, February 18, 1791.

Give the year of their death and place
our presidents are buried.

George Washington died December 14,
1799, buried at Mt. Vernon, Va. The fun-
eral oration was given by Gen. Henry Lee.
John Adams died July 4, 1826. Buried at
Braintree (now called Quincy) near Boston,
Mass. Thomas Jefferson died July 4th,
1826, buried at Monticello, Va. James
Madison died June 28th, 1836. Buried
Montpelier, Va. James Monroe died July
4th, 1831. Buried at Richmond, Va. John
Quincy Adams died Feb. 23, 1848. Buried
at Quincy, Mass. Andrew Jackson died
June 8, 1845. Buried at Hermitage, near
Nashville, Tenn. Martin Van Buren died
July 24, 1862. Buried at Kinderhook, N.
Y. William Henry Harrison died April
4, 1841. Buried fifteen miles west of Cin-
cinnati, Ohio. John Tyler died January
17, 1862. Buried at Hollywood, near
Richmond, Va. Zachary Taylor died July
9, 1850. Buried near Louisville, Ky. Millard Fillmore died March 8, 1874. Buried
near Buffalo, N. Y. Franklin Pierce died
Oct. 8, 1869. Buried at Minot Cemetery,

N. H. James Buchanan died June 1, 1868. Buried at Lancaster, Pa. Abraham Lincoln was assassinated April 14, 1865, at Ford's theatre, Washington City, by John Wilkes Booth. The president is buried at Springfield, Ills. Andrew Johnson died July 31, 1875. Buried at Greenville, Tenn. Ulysses S. Grant died July 23, 1885. Buried at Riverside Park, N. Y. Rutherford B. Hayes died January 17, 1893. Buried at Fremont, Ohio. James A. Garfield was shot by Charles Guiteau at the depot in Washington, D. C., July 2, 1881 and died September 19, 1881. He is buried at Cleveland, Ohio. Chester Allen Arthur died Nov. 18, 1886. Buried at New York City.

What two presidents of the United States died on the same day, just fifty years after the signing of the declaration of independence?

John Adams and Thomas Jefferson both died July 4, 1826.

What is known as the famous "Charter Oak?"

When Connecticut was asked by Sir Edmund Andras to give up her charter, the document was taken away and hid in the hollow of an oak tree, and ever since it has been called the "Charter Oak."

Who founded our Smithsonian institute at Washington, D. C.?

James Smithson, an Englishman, left a legacy to the United States "for the dissemination of knowledge among men."

When did the government establish this institution?

In 1845. It is now a very valuable museum.

When was the census first taken in the United States?

In 1790.

What was the population then?

3,929,214.

Do the members of the British parliament receive any salary?

No.

Who was always known as the "Bachelor President of the United States?"

James Buchanan and Grover Cleveland were the only bachelor presidents we have had. Cleveland married before his term of office expired.

When was the ballot granted the negro in the United States?

Congress proposed the XV amendment of the constitution to the state legislatures Feb. 27, 1869, and by March, 1870, was ratified by thirty of the states, which gave the vote regardless of color.

What is known as the "Original Package decision?"

In the prohibition states the sale of intoxicating liquors was allowed only for mechanical or medicinal purposes. In April, 1890, the supreme court decided that such laws were unconstitutional, so far as they applied to the sale by an importer in original packages of liquors manufactured in and brought from any other state.

What was the "Congress of the Three Americas?"

In October, 1889, representatives of the leading governments of Central and South America, together with the republic of Mexico, met representatives chosen by the United States in a congress held in Washington, D. C.

By what name is it known?

By the name of the "Pan-American Congress."

What was the object of this congress?

To bring about a closer union of Americans, for the purpose of trade and mutual advantage.

How many countries were represented in this congress?

Eighteen. The total number of representatives were 66.

What did the delegates do while here?

They visited the principal commercial and manufacturing cities in the United States. After doing this they returned to Washington and spent the rest of the winter and part of 1890 in discussion of business.

How many officers and employes are engaged in the civil service department?

Nearly 200,000.

FAMILIAR NATIONAL SONGS.

Who wrote the hymn, "My Country, 'tis of Thee?"

Dr. Samuel F. Smith, Feb., 1832.

Who wrote the "Battle Hymn of the Republic?"

Mrs. Julia Ward Howe, Dec., 1861.

Who wrote "Marching through Georgia?"

Henry C. Work in 1865.

Who wrote "Hail Columbia?"

Joseph Hopkinson, in 1798.

Who wrote "The Star Spangled Banner?"

Francis Scott Key, in 1814.

Who wrote "All Quiet Along the Potomac?"

Ethelinda Eliot Beers, in 1861.

Who wrote "Yankee Doodle?"

This is disputed, as it is claimed by many nations.

Who wrote "Tenting on the Old Camp Ground?"

Walter Kittridge, in 1862.

Who wrote "Home, Sweet Home?"

John Howard Payne. He wrote this hymn while a wanderer and living in poverty in 1823.

Who wrote "Maryland, My Maryland?"

James R. Randall, in 1861.

Who wrote "We are Coming, Father Abraham, Three Hundred Thousand Strong?"

The words were written by John Greenlief Whittier during the war, after Lincoln had issued a call for 300,000 more men. A. B. Irving set the words to music and it was sung for the first time in Defiance, Ohio, where it was received with great enthusiasm.

Who wrote the three popular war songs, "Just Before the Battle, Mother," "The Battle Cry of Freedom" and "Tramp, Tramp, the Boys are Marching?"

Mr. Geo. T. Root, Chicago, Ills.

STATE NAMES.

"Liberty and union one and inseperable, now and forever."

What is the origin of the names of the different states?

The names of the Atlantic states are of European origin with the exception of Massachusetts and Connecticut. Most of the other states are of Indian derivation. California and Colorado are taken from the Spanish.

Alabama from the Creek Indian, meaning "here we rest."

Arkansas is taken from the French "arc," a bow, and the Indian word "Kansas," smoky waters, meaning "a bow of smoky waters." It is called the "Bear State."

California means "hot furnace," and on account of the gold is called the "Golden State."

Colorado is from the Spanish and means red, or colored. The name was first given to the Colorado river on account of the reddish tint of the water. It is called the "Centennial State."

Connecticut, from the Indian, Quon-ek-ta-cat, meaning "long river." It is called "Nutmeg State," the "land of steady habits," or the "Free Stone State."

Delaware was named in honor of Lord De la War. It is called the "Diamond State" and "Blue Hen State."

Florida means "Feast of Flowers," and is called the "Peninsular State."

Georgia, so-called after George II of England, and is known as the "Empire State of the South."

Illinois is from the Indian, meaning "A tribe of men," or "manly," and is called the "Prairie" or "Sucker" state.

Indiana, named from the Indians, and is called the "Hoosier State."

Iowa, an Indian name, means "the Sleepy ones." It is styled the "Hawkeye" state.

Kansas, from the Indians, means "Smoky Water." It is called the' 'Garden of the West."

Kentucky signifies "dark and bloody ground." It is called the "Corn Cracker State."

Louisiana, named after Louis XIV of France, is known as the "Creole State" or "Pelican State."

Maine, was originally called "Mayneland. It is termed the "Pine Tree State."

Maryland was named in honor of Henrietta Maria, Queen of Charles I of England.

Massachusetts is from the Massachusetts tribe of Indians, meaning "Blue Hills." It is called the "Old Bay State."

Michigan means "The Lake Country" and is called "Wolverine State."

Minnesota gets its name from the Minnesota River, the Indian meaning "Sky-tinted Water." It is called the "Gopher State."

Mississippi, from the river, the Indian Miche Sepe, meaning "Father of Waters." It is called the "Bayou State."

Missouri, Indian name for river, means "Muddy Water." It is known as "The Pennsylvania of the West."

Nebraska from the Indian, means "Water Valley" or "Shallow River."

Nevada, from the Spanish means, "White as Snow," or "Snow Clad." It is called the "Sage Hen State."

New Hampshire, named by George Mason whose home was formerly in Hampshire Co., England. It is called the "Granite State."

New Jersey was named in honor of Sir George Carterel, one of the governors of the Island of Jersey in the British Channel. It is called "Jersey Blue."

New York was named in honor of the Duke of York, brother of Charles II. It is called the "Excelsior State," and the "Empire State."

North Carolina, named in honor of Charles II. It is called "The Old North State," "The Tar State," and "The Turpentine State."

Ohio, from the Seneca Indians, O—hee—yuh, means "Beautiful River," and is called "The Buckeye State."

Oregon is from the Spanish which means "River of the West.'

Pennsylvania means "Penn's Woods" named in honor of Admiral Penn, father of William Penn. It is called "The Keystone State."

Rhode Island. Authorities differ as to its origin, but an order was given in 1644 which decreed that the Island of Newport should be named the "Isle of Rhodes or Rhode Island." The name afterwards extended to the whole state. It is nicknamed "Little Rhody."

South Carolina, named in honor of King Charles II and is called "The Palmetto State."

Tennessee, from the Indian meaning "The River of the Big Bend." and is called "The Big Bend State."

Texas is from the Aztec, meaning "North Country." Some hold that Texas is Spanish and means "Friends." It is called "The Lone Star State."

Vermont, from the French for green mountains, "vert mont," and is called the "Green Mountain State."

Virginia, named in honor of Elizabeth the Virgin Queen of England. It is called the "Mother of States" and also "The Old Dominion."

West Virginia formed from the western part of the old state of Virginia, nick-named the "Pan handle State."

Wisconsin from Ouisconsin, is the French form of an Indian word which means "A Wild Rushing River." It is called "The Badger State."

Dakota an Indian word meaning "Allies."

Montana, means "Mountainous."

Washington, named after our first president.

OUR NEIGHBORING GOVERNMENTS.
MEXICAN GOVERNMENT.

What is the form of the Mexican Government?

The government of Mexico is modeled after that of the United States.

How is its government divided?

Into three great governmental branches.

What are they?

Their national departments, the Judiciary, and the state governments.

Is the management of these departments the same?

It is substantially the same in all.

How is the national government divided?

Legislative, Executive and Judicial.

How is the Republic of Mexico divided?

Into twenty-seven states. The Territory of Lower California and the Federal District.

What constitutes their national law-making body?

The Federal Congress (or House) and a Federal Senate.

How many members in the Senate?

Fifty-two elected by the states in the State Legislature on the plurality vote.

How many members in the lower House?

227. They are elected by the people on

the basis of the population one for every 80,000 or a major fraction.

How is the President of Mexico elected?

By the people for a term of four years.

Who is Vice-President?

The chief Justice is ex-officio Vice-President.

What is the Capitol?

The city of Mexico, both of the Federal Districts and the Republic.

How is the Supreme Judiciary chosen?

By popular vote for the term of four years.

What language is spoken?

The Spanish.

CANADIAN GOVERNMENT.

What is the form of the Canadian Government?

The form of government is similar to that of their mother country. The constitution is modeled after the British.

How is the Sovereign represented in the Dominion?

By a Governor-General, appointed by the Crown.

How long does he hold office?

During the pleasure of the crown. The constitution provides for the appointment of a council to aid and advise with the Governor-General.

What is this body called?

The Queen's Privy Council. These members represent the majority of the House of Commons.

What constitutes the legislative powers?

They are vested in a Senate and House of Commons.

How are the Senators appointed?

By the Governor-General for life. A Senator must be thirty years of age and own real and personal property to the amount of four thousand dollars above all debts and liabilities.

How many members in the Senate?

There are 80.

How many members in the House of Commons?

There are 215. They are elected for a term of five years.

Where does the Canadian Parliament meet?

At Ottawa.

In the Canadian Parliament there are so many Frenchmen that all bills and motions are read in French as well as in English.

How is Canada divided?

Into seven Provinces; Ontario, Quebec, Nova Scotia, New Brunswick, Manitoba, British Columbia, Prince Edwards Island, and its northtwest Territories.

How are these Provinces governed?

The Governor-General appoints a Lieutenant Governor for each province. He holds office during the pleasure of the Governor-General, unless appointed after the commencement of the first session of Parliament in which case he cannot be removed under five years without a good reason.

Does a province have a legislature?

Each province has its own legislature.

"The clock of time has pealed the woman's hour."   Elizabeth Stuart Phelps.

LIST FOR WOMEN'S CLUBS.

GENERAL LITERATURE. American
Novelists.

American Story-writers.

Character of(the Earliest American
Literature and Writers.

Birth of American Literature.

Our Magazines.

An Afternoon with Poets.

Selections from Longfellow—Evange·
line.

German Literature.

George Elliot as a novelist.

Women in Literature.

ART, MUSIC. The Outlook for Art in
America.

American Artists.

Women Artists of America.

Art in the Public Schools.

English Art.

Italian and Grecian Art, and Artists.

What is Tariff?

Italian Sculpture.

American Sculptors.

Famous American Statues.

American Drama and Dramatists.

History of Music and Musicians of the 19th Century.

Our National Airs.

Woman in Music.

Music in the Public Schools.

EDUCATIONAL. The Founding of Early Colleges.

Higher Education of Women.

The Ethical Influence of women in Education.

Co-Education.

Our Public School system.

Conversation as a fine Art.

The Educational Value of Women's Clubs.

Free Kindergarten as an Economic Factor.

Cultivation of Literary Tastes in Early Life.

After the Diploma—What?

Family Literature.

Good Language in the Home.

Modern Slang.

Manual Training Schools.

HISTORY AND PROGRESS. Classic Greece.

Rome,—B. C.

Queen Anne and the Important Events of Her Reign.

Relation of England to Wales and Ireland.

Victoria as Queen, Wife and Mother.

Russia. Its People, Language and Literature.

Influence of Europe on America.

Washington from the Cradle to the Grave.

Our National Holidays.

Alaska, its people and how governed.

The Chinese and Japanese in America.

Old Spanish Missions in California.

The New South since the War.

How the states received their names.

Panama and Nicaraguan Canal.

Forests and their fate.

American Tramps.

Famous Arctic Explorers.

The Atlantic Cable.

Advancement of Civilization.

The Colonial Period.

CIVIL GOVERNMENT. Our Country's Financial Problem.

National Taxation and Government Bonds.

How were the Colonies Governed?

Continental Congress and Declaration of Independence.

Formation of Federal Constitution.
The Constitution of the United States.
United States Mints.
Our Navy.
Our Postal System.
Civil Service.
Single Tax.
Our Consular Service.
Supreme Court and Jurists.
History of Banks and the Banking System.
History of English and American Coins.
The Australian Ballot.
Reciprocity Treaty.
The Arbitration Treaty.

ECONOMICS. Government ownership of Railroads, Trusts and Monopolies.
Our Monetary System.
Woman in the Home.
Are American Homes Decreasing?
House-keeping in the 20th Century.
Definite School Training for Domestic Service.

SOCIAL SCIENCE, PHILANTHROPY AND REFORMS. The Sweating System.
Conflict of Capital and Labor.
Labor Unions and how they affect the Industrial Classes.
Should Immigration be Restricted?
Recent Socialistic Movements.
Slavery.

Newspapers as an Aid to Philanthropy.

Family versus Institutional Life for Dependent Classes.

Relation of Women's Clubs to Philanthropy.

University Extension and College Settlements.

The Industrial outlook for Women.

Women and Money.

Women as Breadwinners.

Women in Politics.

Woman's Suffrage in Foreign Countries.

Women in Charity and Reform.

SCIENCE. The Theory of Evolution as Taught by Scientists.

What the World owes to Scientific Discoveries in Medicine and Surgery.

Women as Physicians.

Health and Heredity.

The Relation of Vivisection to the Medical Sciences.

Which is greater; Environment or Heredity?

Inventions and Discoveries of the 19th Century.

Geology.

Astronomers and Observatories.

AUTHROPOLOGY, The people of Iceland.

Culture and Work of Mound Builders.
Pueblos and Cliff Dwellers.
Aztics and Mayas.
Women of the Occident in the Orient.
American Indian Tribes.
RELIGIONS. Christianity.
The poetry of the Bible.
Noted Women of the Bible.
The Influence of the Bible on Civilization.
The Mormons.
Judiasm in America.
Judaism B. C.
Martin Luther and the Reformation.
MISCELLANEOUS. Noted Women in the 19th Century.
Are Women Witty?
.omen in Society.
The Art of Entertaining. Its use and abuse.
Pessimism.
Optimism.
Archaeology.

"I say what fine things we have thought of, haven't we, all of us?" —Thackery.

QUOTATIONS FOR CLUB CALENDARS.

"The best we can do for one another is to exchange our thoughts freely, and that, after all, is but little." —Froude.

Man is said to be a sociable animal, and, as an instance of it, we may observe that we take all occasions and pretenses of forming ourselves into those little assemblies which are commonly known by the name of clubs. When a set of men agree in any particular, they form themselves into a kind of fraternity and meet upon account of such fantastic resemblances.— —Addison.

"The union of women for accomplishing high and difficult things is the ladder that raises the climber while it makes the heights accessible."

"As thou, thyself, art a component part of a social system, so let every act of thine be a component part of social life." —Marcus Aurelius Antoninus.

"The delight in good company, in a pure, brilliant social atmosphere in which a wise freedom, an ideal republic of sense, simplicity, knowledge and thorough good meaning abides, doubles the value of life."

"I shower a welcome on you, welcome all."—Shakespeare.

"At Christmas play and make good cheer For Christmas comes but once a year."

".All your strength is in your union, All your danger is in discord."

—Longfellow.

"Use what talents you possess. The woods would be silent if no birds sang but those which can sing best."

"The union for practical progress knows no class, creed, nationality or sex."

All great men are in some degree inspired."—Cicero.

"The first lesson to learn is to be content with simple and common things."

"Reading furnishes the mind only with knowledge. It is thinking makes what we read ours."—Emerson.

"The bee, though it finds every rose has a thorn, comes back loaded with honey from his rambles. And why should not other tourists do the same?" Haliburton.

"A civilization is marked by the completeness of its efforts to rescue those that are lost."

"Some must be great. Great offices will have

Great Talents. And God gives to every man

The virtue, temper, understanding, taste,
That lifts him into life, and lets him fall
Just in the niche he was ordained to fill."
—Cowper.

"So God has ploughed his earth farm
with glaciers to make it ready for the home
of his children."

And he gave it for his opinion, that who-
ever could make two ears of corn, or two
blades of grass, to grow upon a spot of
ground where only one grew before, would
deserve better of mankind and do more es-
sential service to his country, than the
whole race of politicians put together.—
—Dean Swift.

"Men will wrangle for religion, write for
it, die for it; why don't they try to live for
it?"

History is the great looking glass
through which we may behold, with ances-
tral eyes, not only the various deeds of
past ages and the odd accidents that attend
time, but also discover the different hɪ-
mors of men.—Howell.

"The years teach much which the days
never know."—Emerson.

"No past is dead for us, but only sleep-
ing."—Helen Hunt.
"There is no past as long as books shall
live."—Bulwer.

The real object of education is to give children rescources that will endure as long as life endures; habits that time will ameliorate, not destroy; occupation that will render sickness tolerable, solitude pleasant, age venerable, life more dignified and useful, and death less terrible.

—Sidney Smith.

"Who learns, and learns, but acts not what
    he knows,
Is one who ploughs and ploughs, but never
    sows."—Oriental.

"We walk to higher paths by reason's lamp."—George Eliot.

"The University of the world; to which all succeeding ages go to school. Come let us enter the primary."

"We fancy there are many independent sciences, because we stand half way up on different mountain-peaks, calling to each other from isolated stations. The mists hide from us the foot of the range beneath us, or we should see that all the peaks are but offsets of one vast mountain-base, and in their inmost root but One!"

—Charles Kingsley.

Those who give not till they die,
Show that they would not then,
If they could keep it any longer.

—Bishop Hall.

"'Tis the talent of our English nation
Still to be plotting some new reformation."
—Dryden.

Health is the soul that animates all the
enjoyments of life.—Sir W. Temple.

Music is the inarticulate speech of the
heart, which can not be compressed into
words, because it is infinite.—Wagner.

O thou sculptor, painter, poet!
Take this lesson to thy heart,
That is best which lieth nearest,
Shape that from thy work of art.
—Longfellow.

"Art is wonderous long; yet to the wise
her paths are ever fair."—O. W. Holmes.
"In framing artists, art hath thus decreed
To make some good, but others to exceed."
—Shakespeare.

"Painting is silent poetry—and poetry is
a speaking picture."
"What art can with the potter's art com-
pare?
For of what we are ourselves of such we
make our ware."
"True art is never fixed but always flow-
ing."—Emerson.

"A noble farce, wherein kings, republics
and emperors have for so many years played
their parts, and to which the whole vast
universe serves for a theatre."
—Montaigne.

"Transcendent art, exponent of the soul!
Soft shade that marks upon the dial plate
Of every age, how far has climbed the sun
Of man's advancement in the vault of
      thought."

CHILDREN:
Ye the better than all the ballads
   That ever were sung or said,
For ye are living poems,
   And all the rest are dead.

WOMAN. The hand that hath made
you fair hath made you good; the goodness
that is cheap in beauty makes beauty brief
in goodness; but grace, being the soul of
your complexion, should keep the body of
it ever fair.—Shakespeare.

Thy sacred leaves, yon Freedom's Flower,
Shall ever float on dome and tower,
To all their heavenly colors true,
To blackening frost or crimson dew;
And God loves us as we love thee,
Thrice holy Flower of Liberty;
Then hail the banner of the free,
The starry Flower of liberty!
               —Oliver Wendell Holmes.

"'Tis not what man does which exalts
him, but what man would do!"—Browning.

"True civilization is an appreciation of
the rights of others."—E. S. Martin.

"All things are circular: the past,
Was given to make the future great,

And the void future shall at last
Be the strong rudder of an after fate.
God bless the present! It is all;
It has been future, and it shall be past."
                                —Lowell.

"Language is the soil of thought. True vigor and heartiness of phrase do not pass from page to page but from man to man, where the brain is kindle and the lips supplied by down-right living interests."—
                                —Lowell.

"A library may be regarded as the solemn chamber in which a man can take counsel of all that have been wise, and great, and good, and glorious amongst the men that have gone before him."
                                —George Dawson.

"Woman's Empire, holier, more refined,
Moulds, moves and sways the fallen yet
        God breathed mind,
Lifting the earth crushed heart to hope and
        Heaven."—Hale.

"We live in the most wonderful of lands, and one of the most wonderful things in it is, that we as Americans find so little to wonder at.   *   *   *   I hope to live to see Americans proud of knowing America and ashamed not to know it."
                                —Chas. F. Lummis.

"Good-bye," I said, "my dear friends, one and all of you! I have been long with you, and I find it hard parting. I have to thank you for a thousand courtesies, and above all for the patience and indulgence with which you have listened to me, when I have tried to instruct or amuse you. May the Lord bless you all!" And we shook hands all around the table."—

—Holmes.

"It is the glorious prerogative of the empire of knowledge that what it gains it never loses. On the contrary, it increases by the multiple of its own power. All its attainments help to new conquests."—

—Daniel Webster.

"Now gentle reader, is our journey ended, Mute is our minstrel, silent is our song."

—Goethe.

PRACTICAL SUGGESTIONS TO PRES-IDENTS AND MEMBERS OF CLUBS.

Is it necessary for members of a club to understand parliamentary law?

Yes, in order to expedite business and prevent friction.

What is meant by parliamentary law?

Laws which govern deliberative assemblies.

Whence did we derive our parliamentary usage?

From the British parliament.

Why are clubs and conventions often run by a few?

Because a few know parliamentary law and can often carry their points and influence the majority.

THE PRESIDENT.—What are the duties of the presiding officer?

To preside at the meetings, preserve order, put motions to a vote and announce the result.

Should a presiding officer always open the meeting on time?

Yes, if a quorum is present. She should also hold the meeting to the orders of the day in order to finish on time and prevent confusion. Much time is often lost by a presiding officer allowing time to be wasted.

Should a presiding officer have a good knowledge of parliamentary law?

Yes, she should make herself fully acquainted with the rules of order and see that they are enforced. With this knowledge and good common sense, decision and firmness she can keep order and the house strictly to business, always showing with tact and grace consideration for others. She should be prompt,dignified and impartial while in the chair. Be careful to recognize members trying to obtain the floor on either side of the question. Some presiding officers seem to see only the members who think as she does on the question and recognizes and gives them the floor. She can not debate questions while in the chair, but can call some one to preside while she is speaking. She should stand while stating a motion or making explanations; also while taking the vote and should always announce the result. She can vote when her vote will affect the result of the question. If she renders a decision and an appeal is taken she should not show resentment, but put the appeal as any other question, remembering any member has a right to appeal if not satisfied with the decision. She should demand respect for negative opinions, minority votes and majority decisions, even if they do differ from her

own views. After election she should
not feel that she owns the club and everything must go the way she dictates or not at
all. She should not feel when she is elected that she must hold the office for life,
and no one else can fill that place. At the
close of the year, or term of office, she
should not offer her resignation, as her
time is up. And, if, in the election of officers, others are nominated and elected,
she should not feel hurt and refuse to work,
knowing that the best interest of the society is greater than the individual and that
the majority should rule. It is not best for
any organization, as a rule, to keep the
same officers too long. No organization
should be allowed to die for the want of
change in its officers.

THE MEMBERS.—What are the duties
of the members of an organization?

To work with the president for the best
interest of the organization. They should
assist the chair in keeping order.

Is it as important that members understand parliamentary law as it is for the
president?

Yes, because they are the ones to bring
the business before the house and to dispose of the same. They should not think
that the failure or success of the club depends alone on the president. They should
work with and stand by their president,

though she may not be the choice of all. They should be at the opening of the meeting and not keep the president waiting; and if possible, stay until the close. They should attend all the meetings of the club, if possible, and help sustain the interest. They should not come with a poorly written paper if they have had time to give it their best thought and consideration. They should not expect a good club year unless they have given their best efforts to make it such. They should not blame the president with an uninteresting meeting, when some of the members have failed to take the part assigned them. They should not be cynical and always criticise the president when she has put forth her best efforts to make the club year a success. If any member has an ugly disposition and nothing is ever right to her, she should withdraw and give way to one more amiable.

STATE GOVERNMENTS.

It is impossible for us to give here the form of governments of all the states in detail. All the state constitutions are similar, and all must be republican in form and in harmony with the national constitution. The difference between the national and state governments, is, the national government deals with national and exterior affairs, and the state government deals with state, and municipal and interior affairs. Each state has a governor and state legislature. The duty of the governor of the state is similar to that of the president of the United States; but his power is limited to the state. The legislature of the states are almost exactly the same as the national legislature, having two houses, and officered the same. The state governments have the three departments the same as the national—the executive, the legislative and the judicial. James A. Garfield said in speaking of state governments: "It will not be denied that the state government touches the citizen and his interests twenty times where the national government touches him once."

We have selected the state of Ohio as an example of our state governments.

OHIO.

How did Ohio receive its name?

From the Indians calling the river that forms the southeastern boundary "O-hee-yuh," which means "beautiful river."

When was Ohio admitted into the Union?

February 19th, 1803.

What was the form of government previous to the admission?

It was a territory under the control of congress. Congress appointed a governor and three judges, who composed the highest court in the territory.

Where was the first settlement under the authority of congress?

At Marietta, April, 1788.

Whom did congress appoint governor of the territory in 1787?

General Arthur St. Clair.

When was the first territorial legislature chosen?

In 1799. The population had increased so they were entitled to a legislature.

How was the legislature secured?

The electors elected the members of the house, and these members gave ten names to the president of the United States, and he selected five members as the legislative council.

Did the laws passing the legislature at this time have to be approved by the governor?

Yes.

Was the territory represented in congress?

Yes; by a delegate elected by the people.

When was the constitutional convention called to ask for admission?

In 1802, and Ohio was admitted in 1803.

Where did the first general assembly meet?

At Chillicothe, January 11, 1803.

Where did he move to in 1810?

To Zanesville.

When did it move to Columbus?

In 1816.

What is the present capitol of Ohio?

Columbus.

When was the present state house completed?

In 1856. It covers about four and one-half acres of ground.

Who was the first governor of Ohio?

Edward Tiffin.

Name the three divisions of the constitution pertaining to our state government.

Legislative, executive and judicial.

LEGISLATIVE.

What does article II of the state constitution provide?

"The legislative power of this state shall be vested in a general assembly, which shall consist of a senate and house of representatives."

THE HOUSE OF REPRESENTATIVES.—How are the members of the house elected?

By the people.

How is the state divided?

Into eighty-eight counties.

How is the basis of representation determined?

Every ten years the population of the state is divided by one hundred, and each county is entitled to one representative for each ratio. If a county has a population equaled to one-half the ratio, it is entitled to one representative.

What is done with the counties where the population is less than one-half the ratio?

It is placed in a representative district with one of the adjoining counties having the smallest population.

When are the members of the house elected?

At the general state election, which is

held the first Tuesday after the first Monday in November.

For how long a term are the representatives elected?

For two years.

How often are these elections held?

Every two years (the odd numbered years, as 1895, 1897, etc.)

Does our legislature meet every year?

No: every two years, unless there are special sessions called by the governor.

When does the legislature convene?

The first Monday of January, at ten A. M., in the even numbered years.

How many members are there in the House?

One hundred and nine—in1898.

What salary is paid our representatives?

Six hundred dollars a year, and twelve cents per mile for traveling expenses.

ORGANIZATION OF THE HOUSE.—Who calls the house to order?

The secretary of state or the auditor of state?

After calling the house to order what is done?

The house then proceeds to elect one of its own members as presiding officer.

What is he called?

The speaker of the house.

Besides electing the speaker, who else is elected?

A speaker pro tempore.

Is he a member of the house?

Yes.

What officers are elected?

A chief clerk, a messenger clerk, an engrossing clerk, and enrolling clerk, a sergeant-at-arms, three assistant sergeants-at-arms, and pages.

Are these members of the house?

No.

What are the duties of those appointed?

Their duties are similar to those of same offices in the house of congress.

How are the comittees in the house obtained?

They are appointed by the speaker.

Can the speaker vote on all questions?

Being a member of the house he can do so. He also signs all bills passed. After a bill has passed both houses, and has been signed by both presiding officers a copy is sent to the Secretary of State to be preserved. The presenting and passing of bills in the Ohio legislature is similar to that in congress. (See congress.)

Who fixes the ratio of representation?

A board consisting of the governor, auditor and secretary of state.

What is the basis upon which our representatives are elected?

The ratio as fixed in 1891 is one representative for every 36,724.

Which house has the sole right to institute impeachments?

The house of representatives.

THE SENATE.—How many senatorial districts have we?

Thirty-three. Each district has one or more counties.

How is the ratio of representation in the senate known?

The ratio is ascertained by dividing the population of the state by thirty-five. As counted in 1891 it was 104,924; so, for this ratio the district is entitled to a senator.

If a senatorial district has not this full ratio, what is done?

The district is entitled to one senator if it has three-fourths this number of inhabitants.

What is done with districts in which the ratio falls below the required ratio?

It is attached to the adjoining district which has the smallest population.

How many senators have we?

Thirty-six. (1898.)

For how long is a senator elected?

For two years.

How is he elected?

By the electors of the district he represents. He must have been a resident of the district for at least one year.

What salary do senators receive?

Six hundred dollars per year, and twelve cents per mile for traveling expenses.

Who presides in the senate?

The lieutenant governor, by virtue of his office, is president of the senate. He opens the senate the first Monday of January at ten o'clock a. m., and after appointing a clerk pro tempore the roll of the senatorial districts is called, after which the senators present their credentials of election, and take the oath of office.

What is then done?

A speaker pro tempore is elected from among the senators, who will preside in the absence of the president.

What other officials are elected?

A chief clerk, a journal clerk, a messenger clerk, an engrossing clerk, an enrolling clerk, a recording clerk, a sergeant-at-arms and four assistant sergeants-at-arms.

How are the standing committees obtained?

They are elected by the senate.

Can the president of the senate vote?

Not being a member he can vote only when there is a tie.

Does the president sign all bills passed in both houses?

Yes.

How are bills headed?

"Be it enacted by the general assembly of the State of Ohio."

For duties of the clerks, pages, committees, etc., presenting and passage of bills, see Congress, page 17, as they are similar.

THE EXECUTIVE DEPARTMENT.

What provision does the constitution make for the executive department of the state?

That, "the executive department shall consist of governor, lieutenant governor, secretary of state, auditor of state and an attorney general, who shall be elected on the first Tuesday after the first Monday of November by the electors of the state, and at the places of voting for members of the general assembly."

What other offices, whose incumbents are elected by the people, have been created by the general assembly?

The offices of commissioner of common schools, members of the board of public works and the food and dairy commission. There are other offices in the state, but they are appointive.

When do the officers mentioned in the constitution enter upon their official duties?

The second Monday in January after their election.

For how long are they elected?

For a term of two years, except the auditor, who serves for four years. The governor, lieutenant governor, auditor, treasurer and attorney general are chosen in the odd-numbered years, and the secretary of state in the even-numbered years.

THE GOVERNOR.—The constitution says: "The supreme executive power of the state shall be vested in the governor."

How is he elected?

By the electors of the state.

For how long a time is he elected?

For two years.

What salary does he receive?

Eight thousand dollars.

What are his powers and duties?

His duties are to see that the laws are faithfully executed. "He shall communicate at every session by message to the general assembly the condition of the state and recommend such measures as he shall deem expedient." He can call extra sessions of the general assembly on extraordinary occasions. He is commander-in-chief of the military and naval forces of the state, except when they are called into the service of the United States. He commissions all officers of the militia and appoints his own staff. He has the power, after conviction, to grant reprieves, commutations and pardons for all crimes and offenses, except treason, and in cases of impeachment. He can only grant pardons after the board of pardons have reported on the case. He can adjourn the general assembly, if both houses disagree upon an adjournment. He is the custodian of the seal of the state and affixes it to all grants and commissions issued in the name of the state, and all other documents so required by law. A general record of all official acts, proceedings and appointments are kept in the governor's office.

In case of vacancies in the offices of auditor, treasurer, secretary of state or attorney general, how is the office filled.

By appointment from the governor.

Has the governor the veto power.

No; Ohio is one of the four states in which the governor is not vested with this power.

What are the other three states?

Rhode Island, Delaware and North Carolina.

If the governor's office is vacant, or he is unable to perform his duties, who fills the office?

The lieutenant governor.

What salary does the lieutenant governor receive?

Eight hundred dollars per year.

THE SECRETARY OF STATE.—For how long is the Secretary of State chosen?

For two years.
What bond must he give?
$100,000.

What are his duties?

He is the custodian of the official copies of all laws and resolutions that have been passed by the legislature, and of all reports of the executive and judicial departments. He, also, must see that correct copies are prepared for publication, and he distributes them as provided by law. All statistics collected and reported by township assessors, school directors and prosecuting attorneys are kept by him and from these he publishes, annually, the statistics concerning the public and business interests of the state. He, also, provides the seals of office which the governor, judges and all other officers are required by law to use. He is the state sealer of weights and measures. All articles of incorporation for associations and societies must be filed in his office. He provides these forms of incorporation. He is supervisor of elections, and furnishes to each county and voting district in the state, ballots to be used in state elections, and after the elections he publishes the returns. All commissions issued by the governor are signed by him. He purchases and distributes all official stationery for the use of state officers and members of the legislature.

What salary does he receive?

$4,000 per year.

THE AUDITOR OF STATE.—For how long a time is the Auditor of State chosen?

For four years.

What bond is he required to give?

$20,000.

What are his duties?

He is the bookkeeper of the state. He must keep a full account of all financial transactions of the state government. Money can only be paid out of the state treasury by an order from him. He must examine the condition of the state treasury quarterly and report to the governor.

What salary does he receive?

$3,000 per year.

THE TREASURER OF STATE.—For how long a time is the treasurer of the state chosen?

For two years.

What is he required to do before entering upon his official duties?

To give a bond acceptable to the governor in the sum of $600,000. He receives and pays out the money for the state upon orders issued by the auditor of state. He publishes monthly statements of the condition of the treasury and makes annual reports of all money received and paid out.

What salary does he receive?

$3.000 per year.

THE ATTORNEY GENERAL. — For how long a time is the Attorney General elected?

For two years.

What bond must he give?

$5,000.

What are his duties?

He is the legal adviser of all the executive officers of the state, and of the directors of the state public institutions and of the questions submitted to the state legislature. He is also the prosecuting attorney of all the counties. That is, he prosecutes cases in the supreme court in which the state is a party. He represents the state in the lower courts when required to do so by the governor. When required by the governor, state legislature or other proper authority, he brings suit against state officers for not doing their duty.

What salary does he receive?

His salary is $1,500, and fees amounting to about $1,500.

THE COMMISSIONER OF PUBLIC SCHOOLS.—For how long a time is the commissioner of public schools elected?

For a term of three years.

What bond does he give?

$5,000.

When does he enter upon his official duties?

The second Monday in July following his election.

What are his duties?

He is required by law to visit annually each judicial district in the state, and confer with boards of education, encourage teachers' institutes, counsel teachers, visit schools, etc., etc. He represents to the legislature the condition and needs of the common schools of the state.

What salary does he receive?

$2,000 per year and traveling expenses.

THE BOARD OF PUBLIC WORKS.—How many members constitute the board of public works?

There are three. One is elected every year, and they serve for a term of three years.

What great enterprise has been accomplished through this board?

Two great canals have been built. One from Cleveland to Portsmouth, and one from Toledo to Cincinnati. These canals are under their supervision. They fix the toll rates and appoint toll collectors and

lock tenders. The chief engineer is ap
pointed by the governor.

What bond is required of each member?
$30,000.

MINOR EXECUTIVE OFFICERS. —
There are a great many minor officers and
boards, appointed by the governor, with
the consent of the senate, such as a board
of pardons, consisting of four members;
board of school examiners, five members,
serving five years; state board of agriculture, twelve members, and serving two
years. Of agricultural experiment stations there are three members, serving
three years, and of the forestry bureau
there are three members, serving six years.
The commissioner of labor statistics serves
two years. The board of state charities is
composed of the governor and seven other
members appointed by him, to serve three
years. A commissioner of railroads and
telegraphs, serving two years; canal commissioners, two, serving two years; a board
of pharmacy, five members, serving eight
years; a state geologist; commissioners of
public printing, the secretary of state, the
auditor of state and the attorney general;
commissioners of sinking fund are also the
secretary of state, the auditor of state and
the attorney general; a board of arbitration, three members, serving three years;
a board of dental examiners, five members,

serving three years; a free employment bureau, five superintendents, serving two years; inspector of mines, one chief inspector, serving four years, and seven assistant inspectors, serving three years; inspector of work shops and factories, one chief inspector, serving four years, and eleven district inspectors, serving three years; supervisor of public printing and binding, two years; state library, the governor, secretary of state and the state librarian; the state librarian, serving two years; live stock commissioners, three members, serving three years. The dairy food commissioner, since 1891, has been an elective instead of an appointive office; elected for two years. The superintendent of insurance and inspector of buildings and Loan associations serves three years; inspector of oils, two state inspectors, serving two years, and thirty deputies, serving two years; state board of veterinary examiners, three members, serving six years; meteorological bureau, three members.(Some of the members of these department executives of the state are ex-officio members.)

How are our state institutions controlled?

By a State Board of Control.

THE JUDICIARY.

What is meant by the judiciary department.

The constitution says: "The judicial power of the state shall be vested in a supreme court, circuit courts, courts of common pleas, courts of probate, justices of the peace and such other courts, inferior to the supreme court, as the general assembly may from time to time establish."

What is the duty of the legislative department?

To make laws, and it is the duty of the Judicary to interpret them and to declare what is and what is not constitutional law. And in order to have this done the judicial department consists of a system of courts.

What is a court?

It is an organized tribunal established to administer the laws for the people. These courts are composed of one or more judges.

How are the cases brought for trial?

By attorneys. The clerks of the courts must record the acts and decisions.

What is a case before the court called?

A suit or law suit. They are either civil or criminal.

The court proper is composed of how many classes of judges?

Two; the judge and jury.

What is a jury?

A number of men secured according to law to inquire into and to determine the facts concerning a case submitted to them, and to render a decision upon the evidence stated. When a case is heard before a jury, the court, or judge, states to the jury the law relating to the case. This is called charging the jury. The jury then is to find a verdict in harmony with the facts and law.

What classes of jury have we?

The grand jury and the petit jury.

What is a civil case?

A suit brought to recover a debt, damages or to secure civil rights. Civil cases are brought by the injured person or persons.

What is a criminal suit?

A criminal suit is brought to convict a person of crime. In criminal cases the suit is brought in by the state, represented by officers chosen, the officers being the grand jurors and the prosecuting attorney.

How are juries secured?

The statutes declare that at the first term of each year the common pleas court of each county shall determine the number of persons necessary to be selected from each county annually to serve as petit jurors and grand jurors in the various courts of the county.

Who appoints the number determined upon among the townships and city wards?

The clerk of the court.

When is the appointment of these persons made?

On election day the township trustees and city councilmen select the required number of persons, and the selections are reported to the clerk of the court.

What is then done?

The clerk writes the names on separate pieces of paper and drops them into a box provided for that purpose. The number in the box is always in excess of the number of jurors required.

When are the names drawn out?

At a certain time before each term of court opens the clerk draws from the box, in the presence of the sheriff, twenty-seven names.

How are these to be divided?

Fifteen for grand jurors and twelve for petit jurors.

Who summons the persons thus selected?

The sheriff.

At the beginning of the trial the parties, through their attorneys, may question the jurors thus selected, and if any objections are found they are excused and the sheriff summons some by-stander to take his place.

What compensation do jurors and witnesses receive?

Jurors in common pleas courts receive $2.00 per day. Witnesses receive one dollar per day and five cents per mile each way. If there is a jury in the jnstice of tne peace court trial they are paid seventy-five cents per day each, and the witnesses are paid fifty cents per day.

THE TRIAL.—What is the party bringing the suit called?

The plaintiff.

The party against whom the suit is brought is called what?

The defendant.

Who presents the case to the court?

The attorneys employed by both parties, unless it is a case where the state is the plaintiff, such as criminal cases. Then the prosecuting attorney represents the interests of the state.

Describe a trial by jury.

The statutes provide as follows: A jury is secured and sworn in. Then the plaintiff states his claim and briefly states the evidence by which he expects to sustain it. The defendant then briefly states his defense and the evidence he expects to offer in support of it. Witnesses of the plaintiff are sworn in and examined by the counsel for the plaintiff, after which they may be cross-examined by the counsel of the defendant. The counsel of the defendant presents his witnesses, each one is examined, then both the plaintiff and the defendant presents to the jury arguments in favor of their side of the question, and the judge of the court instructs the jurors, after interpreting the law as applied to the case, and the jurors retire.

The jurors must be kept together in some convenient place under the charge of an officer, until they agree upon a verdict, or are discharged by the court, subject to the discretion of the court to permit them to separate temporarily at meals. The officer having them in charge shall not suffer any communication to be made to them or make any himself except to ask them if they have agreed upon their verdict, unless by order of the court.

What is done if the jury disagree?

The judge dismisses the case and it stands as if it had not been tried.

If they agree and a verdict is returned, what is done?

The verdict is reduced to writing and signed by the foreman; the jurors are then taken to the court room, their names called by the clerk, and the verdict rendered by the foreman, then the clerk reads the verdict to the jury and inquires whether it is their verdict. If it is a civil case the judge orders the sheriff to enforce the verdict. If it is a criminal case the judge pronounces sentence against the accused and directs the sheriff to carry it into effect.

What is the highest court in the state?

The supreme court.

How many judges has it?

Six, one elected each year, and who serves a term of six years.

When does their term begin?

In February next after their election.

Who is the chief justice?

Each year the judge whose term of office has most nearly expired becomes the chief justice of the state.

What is the salary of the judges of the supreme court?

$4,000 a year.

When does the term of the supreme court open?

In January, beginning the Tuesday after the first Monday.

Where is it held?

In Columbus.

What number is necessary to render a decision?

A majority.

How is the clerk of the supreme court elected?

By the people of the state, for a term of three years.

What is done if a case is brought from a lower court and the supreme court is evenly divided?

The decision of the lower court is regarded as final.

What is meant by the jurisdiction of the supreme court?

It means that it has power to hear and examine 'cases. It is both original and appellate.

What is meant by original?

That a case or suit must begin in that court.

What is meant by appellate jurisdiction?

When a case is carried up from a lower to a higher court, for the sake of having the decision of the lower court re-examined.

Does the supreme court have a jury?

No; and no new evidence as to the facts in the case is admitted. The supreme court either affirms the decision of the lower court, modifies or reverses it, or sends the case back to be tried again.

Is the decision of the state Supreme Court final?

Yes; except where the constitution and laws of the United States are involved. In such cases an appeal may be taken to the United States supreme court.

Are all decisions published?

Yes; the court has a reporter who prepares the decisions for publication.

THE CIRCUIT COURT.—How is the state divided?

The counties of the state are grouped into eight judicial circuits, with one circuit court in each.

How many judges in each circuit?

Three; one elected biennially for a term of six years. They are elected by the voters. The circuit courts have both appellate and original jurisdiction. The main work of the circuit court is the rehearing of the cases on appeals or errors from the next lower court.

How many terms of court are held a year?

There must be two terms of court held every year in each county.

How are the terms fixed?

The third Tuesday of September the circuit judges meet at Columbus and fix the time for the court to meet in each county, and the clerks of the courts are thus in-

formed. This order is recorded and published in the newspapers.

What salaries do these judges receive?

$4,000 a year.

THE COURTS OF COMMON PLEAS.—
How many common pleas districts are
there in the state?

The state is divided into ten common
pleas districts, and if they contain three or
more counties they are divided into three
sub-divisions each.

How are the judges elected?

By the sub-districts, the number being
fixed by law.

How long do they serve?

For a term of five years.

Has this court original and appellate
jurisdiction?

Yes; a great many cases of importance
begin here, and cases are appealed from
lower courts to this.

How many terms are held each year?

There must be at least three sessions
held in each county every year.

What salaries do these judges receive?

$2,500 a year each, except where the leg-
islature authorizes an extra salary in some
districts where the work is very heavy.
The extra salaries are paid by the county.

In Hamilton county the judges receive $6,-000 and in Cuyahoga county $5,000.

THE JUSTICE OF THE PEACE AND THE MUNICIPAL COURTS.—How are Justices of the Peace elected?

By the electors in the township in which they live. The state is divided into townships and each township has one or more justices of the peace.

What authority has a justice of the peace?

To try civil cases involving small amounts. He can cause the arrest of persons suspected of committing crime, and if guilty either have them sent to jail or put under bond for their appearance in the next term of the court of common pleas.

What is the lowest of all the courts?

That which is held by the justice of the peace. He tries many cases of petty offences.

Has the justice of the peace any authority outside of the township in which he is elected?

No.

For how long a term are justices of the peace elected?

Three years.

What courts besides these are held in cities and villages?

Mayor's or police courts, where persons

are tried for petty offenses.

What provision does the constitution make for probate courts?

The constitution says: "The probate court shall have jurisdiction in probate and testamentary matters, the appointment of administrators and guardians, the settlement of the accounts of executors, administrators and guardians, and such jurisdiction in habeas corpus, and the issuing of marriage licenses, and for the sale of land by executors, administrators and guardians, and such other jurisdiction, in any county or counties, as may be provided by law."

How many probate courts have we in the state?

Eighty-eight. One in each county.

How many probate judges have we?

Eighty-eight. One for each county. They are elected for a term of three years.

What special act passed the state legislature in March, 1896?

An act creating for Cuyahoga county a court of insolvency, with a judge elected for five years, and who receives the same salary as the probate judge of the county, $5,000.

THE MILITIA.—What is the state militia?

It is a military organization of the state.

What provision does the constitution make pertaining to the militia?

That "all white male citizens, residents of this state, being eighteen years of age, and under the age of forty-five years, shall be enrolled in the militia, and perform military duty, in such manner, not incompatible with the constitution and laws of the United States, as may be prescribed by law."

What does the above statute mean?

That although all persons are enrolled, they are only liable to be pressed into service in case of war.

Have we an organized militia in the state?

Yes; the Ohio National Guards, composed of volunteers of military age, enlisting for five years.

Who are exempt from this law?

Idiots, lunatics, convicts and persons whose religious faith prevent them from going to war or carrying arms.

Who is commander of the state military forces?

The governor, except when they are called out in the United States service.

What appointments for the militia are made by the governor?

The adjutant general, quartermaster-general and such other officers as are provided for by law.

Who is the chief of the governor's staff?

The Adjutant General.

STATE INSTITUTIONS.—What of the state institutions?

Ohio has a great many state institutions, such as educational, penal, reformatory and institutions for the unfortunate.

How are these institutions supported?

By the state.

How are the appointments of these institutions made?

By the trustees, and confirmed by the governor.

EDUCATION.—What provision does the state constitution make for our public schools?

It says: "The general assembly shall make such provision by taxation and oth· erwise, as, with the income arising from the school trust fund, will secure a thorough and effective system of comon schools throughout the state; but no religious or other sect, or sects, shall ever have any exclusive right to, and control of, any part of the school funds of the state."

How is the state divided?

Into small school districts, so that all may have the advantage of the free public schools.

How is the money raised to support our public schools?

By tax, mostly.

Who is the official head of the public schools in the state?

The state commissioner of common schools.

When was the law passed granting woman suffrage in school elections?

In 1894.

INCORPORATIONS.—What is meant by incorporations?

It means the binding together, or uniting in one body.

What are the first steps to incorporate?

The statutes say: "Any number of persons, not less than five, a majority of whom are citizens of this state, desiring to become incorporated, shall subscribe and acknowledge, before an officer authorized of take acknowledgments of deeds, articles of incorporation, the form of which shall be prescribed by the secretary of state."

What must these articles contain if for profit?

First, the name of the corporation; second, where the corporation is to be located; third, the purpose of said corporation, and the number of shares into which the stock is divided.

If it is for non-profit, what do the articles contain?

First, the name of the association; second, where located or place of principal business, together with the names and residences of the principal officers; third, the purpose of the incorporation.

What is then done?

A charter is issued to the persons named in the application for the incorporation.

ELECTIONS.—What is meant by an elector?

Every male citizen of the United States of the age of twenty-one years—and women when they vote.

How long must they be residents of the state?

One year, and thirty days in county; and in the township, village or ward, twenty days.

Who are prohibited by the constitution from voting?

Persons convicted of bribery, perjury, crime, also idiots and insane people.

Can women vote in Ohio?

Only on the school question.

How are the candidates for office nominated?

By the political parties at nominating conventions, and at the primaries.

What are primaries?

By primaries is meant the meetings of the members of a political party in a district or precinct to nominate candidates for office or to elect delegates to a convention. The law prescribes how the primaries shall be held and the committees of the party fixes the dates.

What is a nominating convention?

A convention of chosen delegates to nominate candidates.

How are candidates chosen?

Sometimes in primaries and sometimes in conventions. County officers are chosen usually at a delegated convention—delegates chosen in primaries in the township and in city wards.

How are the state officers chosen?

By a delegated convention composed of delegates chosen from the counties.

How are the state senators nominated?

By senatorial district conventions composed of delegates.

How is the President and Vice-President of the United States nominated?

By a nominating convention of delegates from the states.

To how many delegates is each state entitled in a National Convention?

To twice as many delegates as it has members in Congress. Ohio is entitled to forty-six delegates.

How are the delegates elected?

Four are elected at the state convention and are called delegates-at-large and the others are elected by the congressional conventions in the state.

Are the territories represented in National conventions?

Usually two or more are admitted from each territory.

Who is at the head of the elections in the state?

The State Supervisor of Elections.

Who is this?

By virtue of his office the Secretary of State. He controls all elections except for school directors and road supervisors.

Who appoints the county board of Deputy State Supervisors?

The State Supervisor of Elections appoints for each county four members as the board of elections. They are appointed on or before the first Monday of August, two biennially and for a term of four years.

When do these deputy supervisors meet and organize?

They meet at the county commissioners office at least thirty days before the November election and choose one of the members for clerk and one for president.

What are the duties of these deputies?

They must appoint, annually, judges and clerks of elections for every voting precinct. The law requires that they "shall advertise and let the printing of ballots, cards of instruction and other required books and papers to be printed by the county." They see that each precinct is provided with ballots, also poll books, tally-sheets and other required books and papers belonging to each polling place. They must, also, see that suitable polling places are provided for the voters according to law.

Can a person who is a candidate serve as a judge or clerk of elections?

No.

How many officers are required at each election precinct?

The board of deputy state supervisors, at least ten days before the election, appoints for each precinct four judges and two clerks, (except in cities where the voters must register where they are appointed by the city board of elections.) There cannot be more than two judges and one clerk belonging to the same political party.

Do all judges and clerks have to take the oath of office?

Yes.

Can a judge or clerk challenge a voter as to his right to vote?

Yes.

What are the duties of the judges and clerks?

They, on the day of election, receive and count the ballots and send in the returns.

What compensation do these judges receive?

For meeting the county board, receiving the ballots, blanks, and papers to hold an election, the presiding judge receives two dollars, and, also, five cents per mile traveling to and from the county seat; and those carrying in the returns receive the same. The judges and clerks of elections receive three dollars for each election. For compensation of judges and clerks in cities of the first and second class see revised statutes.

REGISTRATION OF VOTERS.—What is required of cities of the first and second class?

The electors must register annually before the November election.

How is this done?

The board of elections appoint two of the judges of each precinct of different parties, and on certain days electors must register to be entitled to vote.

NOTICE OF ELECTION.--What is required of the sheriff of each county before election?

Fifteen days before the November election he issues a proclamation throughout the county, of the time, and place of holding the election and officers to be voted for.

How is this done?

He is required to post copies of his proclamation at the polling places and publish it in the newspaper.

How are municipal elections announced?

In a similar way only by the mayor instead of the sheriff.

How are the township elections announced?

By the trustees, the constable posting the notices in the polling places.

When is the state and county election day for electing members of Congress, the President, and all state and county officers?

The first Tuesday after the first Monday in November.

When are the township and municipal officers elected?

The first Monday in April.

AUSTRALIAN BALLOT.—What is our present system of voting?

The Australian and is known to us as the Australian Ballot. It was first used in Australia in 1857.

When was it first used in this county?

In 1888 it was used in St. Louis, Ky., and in some places in Mass.

Have all states adopted this system of voting?

Nearly all.

What advantage has the present system over the old way of voting?

Now every voter can deposit a secret ballot and he avoids intimidation.

At what hour on election day are the polls declared opened?

At 5:30 a. m. (standard time) the presiding judge of election declares the polls open and at 5:30 p. m. they are closed except in Cincinnati where they are closed at 4 p. m.

How are the voting places arranged?

The law requires the room in which the election is to be held to be divided into two parts by a railing. One place for the election officers and the ballot box and the other part is made into closets called voting booths.

What is the first thing an elector does upon entering the voting place?

He gives his name and address to the officer and if his name is on the register's or assessor's book he is given an official ballot.

What is on the ballot?

The names of the candidates of all the different parties. These are arranged in seperate columns. No ballots but those prepared and provided by law can be used.

What does the elector do next?

He retires to one of the voting booths and, in private, prepares his ballot.

Can two persons occupy the same booth at the same time?

No.

How long is he allowed to prepare his ballot?

Five minutes.

With what must all marks be made?

With a black lead pencil.

If the elector spoils the first ballot what can he do?

Secure others, one at a time, until he has had three.

What becomes of the soiled ballots?

They are delivered to the officers and immediately destroyed.

If the elector is unable to mark his own ballot what can he do?

Ask for assistance. Then two judges of different political parties help him mark it or mark it for him.

If the elector wants to vote "a straight ticket," (that is for every candidate of his political party,) how does he mark his ballot?

He makes a cross (x) within the circle at the head of the column containing the names of all the candidates of his party. If he wishes to vote a "mixed ticket" or for only a part of the ticket how does he mark his ballot?

He makes a cross (x) opposite the names of the candidates for whom he wishes to vote.

If the elector wishes to vote for any person whose name does not appear on the ticket can he do so?

Yes, by filling in the blank space which is left on the ticket for that purpose.

What then is done with the ballot?

Before leaving the booth the elector folds his ballot so as not to display the marks thereon. The ballot is then given to one of the election officers who detaches the secondary stub bearing the electors registered number or name, and deposits the ballot in the ballot box. The secondary stubs are preserved until the polls are closed and then they are destroyed, before the ballot box is opened, together with the unused ballots.

What is next done?

The judges and clerks must then certify on the poll books the number of electors entered and voted. The presiding judge then proclaims in a loud voice outside the polling room the number of votes so shown on the poll books.

What is then done?

If it is a registered precinct they are checked off on the duplicate registers. The ballot box is then opened and all the ballots are first counted by the judges.

What is done if there are more ballots in the box than the number entered in the poll-books?

One of the judges, with his back to the ballot box, and without seeing, draws out and destroys the number equal to the excess.

How are the ballots counted?

One of the judges takes the ballots from the box, one at a time and reads aloud, while the ballot is in his hand, all the names on the ballot. He then hands it to the other judges for inspection.

Who keeps the tally-sheet?

The clerks.

After all ballots have been counted what is done?

The tally-sheets are signed by the judges and clerks and returns are made to the proper officers as required by law.

What is done with the ballots after they have been counted?

They are burned by the judges.

THE COUNTY.—How is the state of Ohio divided?

Into sub-divisions, called counties.

How many counties have we?

Eighty-eight.

What is the county seat of a county?

It is where the court house is located and the important official business of the county is transacted.

What are the county officers?

Commissioners, auditor, treasurer, re-corder, surveyor, infirmary directors, clerk of courts, sheriff, coroner, prosecuting at-torney and probate judge.

When does the election of these officers take place?

The constitution says: "County officers shall be elected on the first Tuesday after the first Monday in November by the elect-ors of each county in such manner, and for such term, not exceeding three years, as may be provided by law."

When these officers are elected, what are they required to do?

To take the oath of office and give bond.

Who gives them a certificate of election?

The governor.

THE COUNTY COMMISSIONERS.— How many commissioners has each county?

Three; one member being chosen each year, and the term of office is for three years.

How often are they required to meet?

Once in three months at the county seat.

What are their duties?

To look after the condition of our roads and ditches and build and repair bridges. They have supervision of county property. They are required to furnish and maintain a court house, a jail, an infirmary, and furnish offices for the county officers. They must let the contracts for erection of county buildings, furnishings, repairs, etc. It is their duty to make the levy of taxes for the support of the county.

What salaries do county commissioners receive?

In most counties they receive $3.00 per day for working days, but in some counties there is a fixed annual salary.

Who is the secretary of the board?

The county auditor.

What bond are the commissioners required to give?

Not less than $5,000.

THE TREASURER.—How is the treasurer elected?

By the electors, for a term of two years.

What are his duties?

He collects all taxes and pays out the money from the county treasury. If tax payers do not pay their taxes he causes the property to be advertised and sold at public sale for same. He must keep his accounts open to the inspection of the commissioners.

What salary does he receive?

It is not the same in all counties, and it depends upon the amount of taxes collected, as he gets a percentage.

What bond must he give?

This is directed by the county commissioners.

THE COUNTY AUDITOR.—How is the county auditor elected?

By the electors, for a term of three years.

What are his duties?

He is the bookkeeper of the county, and must keep the account of all money received and paid out by the county treasurer. Money can only be paid out of the treasury by warrants issued by the auditor. He must make a list of all taxable property in the county, as furnished by the assessors. He must furnish county treasurers duplicate tax lists. By virtue of his office he is county sealer of weights and measures. The auditor and treasurer must make settlements twice a year.

What bond does he give?

Not less than $5,000.

THE RECORDER.—How is the recorder elected?

By the electors of the county, for a term of three years.

What are his duties?

He must keep the official copies of all legal papers pertaining to the transfer of houses and lands. He records mortgages, looks after the titles of land, and when land is sold the deeds are recorded by him at the county seat.

Does he receive a stated salary?

No; he is paid by those transacting business with him, who have papers recorded.

What bond is he required to give?

$2,500.

THE COUNTY SURVEYOR.—How is the county surveyor elected?

By the electors, for a term of three years.

What are his duties?

He must make all surveys of lands when the boundaries are disputed in court, un- less the parties or court agree upon some one else. He must survey all lands that are sold for taxes. County roads, ditches and bridges, etc., are surveyed by him.

What bond is he required to give?

Two thousand dollars, with two or more securities to the satisfaction of the county commissioners.

What salary does he receive?

He receives as salary whatever is order- ed by the county commissioners for his work.

THE INFIRMARY DIRECTORS.— How are the Infirmary directors elected?

In counties where they have infirmaries, or county poor houses supported by the county, the electors of the county elect three directors, one each year, to serve a term of three years.

What are the duties of these directors?

To look after the general management of the infirmary. To appoint a superintend- ent and fix his salary. They usually ad- mit paupers to the infirmary upon infor- mation of the trustees of the township. The directors make the rules that govern the institution. They must make semi-an- nual reports to the county commissioners.

What salary do they receive?

Two dollars and fifty cents for every day devoted to official work.

What bond do they give?

Not less than $2,000, nor more than $30,000.

THE CORONER.—How is the coroner elected?

By the electors, for a term of two years.

What are his duties?

When the body of a person whose death is supposed to have been caused by violence, is found in the county, it is reported to the coroner, and he must hold an "inquest," or examination, for the purpose of finding out how the person met with death. He has the power to issue subpoenas for witnesses, if necessary. If he finds that death was caused by another person he can cause such person to be placed under arrest and brought to trial.

What salary does he receive?

For each inquest he is allowed three dollars and all the necessary expenses; but in all counties containing a city of the second or third class, the coroner is paid, in lieu of fees, a salary of two thousand dollars a year.

What bond does he give?

Not less than $5,000, nor more than $50,-

000. The sum is fixed by the county commissioners.

THE SHERIFF.—For how long is the sheriff elected?

For two years.

What are his duties?

As he is the ministerial officer of the courts, he or a deputy must attend the court of common pleas and circuit courts. He must preserve the public peace and cause the arrest of all offenders against it, and cause them to be brought to trial. He serves all subpoenas issued to witnesses, except those issued by justices of the peace. He has charge of prisoners on trial and of the witnesses, and summons jurors. He has charge of the county jail and prisoners. He must always serve notice or issue a printed proclamation of all general elections. He must conduct the sale of property when it has been ordered to be sold for debts.

What salary does he receive?

He has no stated salary, but is paid by fees for the various duties he must perform, or the amount of business done.

What bond must he give?

Not less than $5,000, nor more than $50,-000, which is fixed by the county commissioners.

THE CLERK OF THE COURTS.—For
how long is the clerk of the courts elected?

For a term of three years.

What are his duties?

He must act as clerk of the court of common pleas, and the circuit court of the
county. The clerk must enter all orders,
decrees, judgments and proceedings of the
courts, and must make a complete record
of every case tried in both of the courts.
He has power as clerk to administer oaths
and take and certify affidavits, and deposi-
tions, and acknowledgements of deeds and
mortgages. He must make an annual report to the secretary of state of the
cases tried in the courts.

What salary does he receive?

He is paid by fees for the various kinds
of work done.

THE PROSECUTING ATTORNEY.—
For how long is the prosecuting attorney
elected?

For three years.

What are his duties?

As prosecuting attorney he must prosecute, on behalf of the state, in any of the
courts of the county (except the justice's
courts) all suits, matters and controver-
sies, as directed by law. He must prepare
in legal form the official bonds for the
county officers and see that they are prop-

erly signed. He is also the legal adviser of all county officers, and he must make an annual report to the state attorney general of all crimes prosecuted in the county.

What bond is he required to give?

Not less than a thousand dollars, the sum to be fixed by the courts.

What salary does he receive?

It is not the same in all counties.

THE PROBATE JUDGE.—For how long is the probate judge elected?

For three years.

What are his duties?

To transact the business of the probate court. (See probate court.)

What salary does he receive?

This depends upon the work done by him in the county. He receives fees.

THE TOWNSHIP.—How are the counties of Ohio divided?

Into townships. Each township is a corporate body and can sue and be sued in the courts in the person of its officers. It can also receive, hold and dispose of real or personal property, borrow money for the use of the township, and taxes may be levied on the township for the expenses of the same.

Who are the officers of the township?

They are the trustees, clerk, treasurer,

justices of the peace, constables, assessors and road supervisors.

When are these township officers elected?

The first Monday of April of each year.

THE TRUSTEES.—For how long are the trustees elected?

There are three trustees in each township, elected for three years.

What are their duties?

They transact the official business of the township. They represent the township in suits at law; they look after public property, determine the amount of money necessary for the expenses of the township and levy an annual tax for the same. They look after the paupers; they may order new roads and ditches made; they have charge of the township's cemeteries; they must provide town halls and a public library, if the electors of the township, by vote, order it.

What compensation do they receive?

They are paid a fixed sum for each day they work for the township.

THE CLERK.—For how long is the township clerk elected?

For two years.

What are his duties?

He must keep a record of all the proceedings of the board of trustees.. He keeps a record with description of roads and ditches. All the records, books, and papers of the township are kept by him. He keeps an account of all official debts, receipts and expenditures of the trustees. He places on file all chattel mortgages given in the township. He is also the clerk of the township school district.

What salary does he receive?

A fee for the amount of work done.

THE TREASURER.—For how long is the township treasurer elected?

For two years.

What are his duties?

He is the custodian of the township funds. The money belonging to the township from taxes collected by the county treasurer are turned over to the township treasurer.

How can he pay out money?

Only on orders drawn by the trustees and countersigned by the clerk. He is also the treasurer of the township school district.

What salary does he receive?

He is allowed two per cent on all money paid out by him.

THE ASSESSOR.—For how long is the assessor elected?

He is elected for one year.

What are his duties?

He must list the value of all personal property in the township subject to taxation. This list must be forwarded to the county auditor, and each person's taxes are made out for the year. He collects facts concerning agriculture, manufactures, and other industrial interests; also business statistics.

What compensation does he receive?

He is paid two dollars for each day's work.

THE CONSTABLE.—For how long is the constable elected?

For three years.

What are his duties?

To preserve peace in the township and arrest all violators of the law. He may be called upon to serve warrants and subpoena witnesses for county courts. He must preserve order at the polling places on election days.

THE SUPERVISOR OF ROADS.—For how long are the supervisors of roads elected.

For one year.

What are their duties?

The trustees of the township divide the township into road districts, and a supervisor is elected for each district. His duties are to open all public roads and highways and keep the same in repair in his district, as ordered by the trustees.

How is the money raised for taking care of our roads?

By taxation. Every male between twenty-one and fifty-five years of age is responsible for two days' work annually on the roads, at the rate of one dollar and fifty cents per day. All of this work is under the direction of the supervisor of the district.

MUNICIPAL CORPORATIONS.--What are the different forms of municipal corporations?

They are the city, village and hamlet.

How are municipal corporations formed?

They are organized under the general state laws which make provision for their form of government and power.

What advantage is it to a community to incorporate?

It has the advantage of local government.

How may a community incorporate?

The inhabitants wishing to incorporate draft a petition, signed by not less than thirty electors, residing within the proposed corporate limit, and the petition is presented to the board of commissioners; then the petition has a hearing at the regular meeting. If, after due consideration, and notice having been given, there is no reason why it should not be granted, the commissioners allow the corporation to organize. The corporation papers, giving name, etc., are recorded, and the time for the first election of officers is fixed by the agents of the petitioners.

HAMLET.—What is a hamlet?

A hamlet is a municipal corporation with less than two hundred population. After being incorporated they have certain rights of governing themselves, such as the right of municipal gas, electric lights, sidewalks, sewers, railways, etc., which may be granted or not by vote of the people.

What are the officers of a hamlet?

Three trustees, a treasurer, a clerk, a marshal and a supervisor of roads. The duties of these officers are nearly the same as the officers in the township. The principal authority of a hamlet is in the board of trustees. When a hamlet has grown to more than two hundred they can be incorporated as a village by vote of the electors.

VILLAGE.—What is a village?

A municipal corporation with a population more than two hundred and less than five thousand, and which has a form of organization to govern themselves in municipal affairs.

In whom is the legislative power vested?

In a council elected by the electors.

Who are the executive officers?

A mayor, a clerk, a treasurer and a marshal.

THE COUNCIL.—What are the duties of the council?

To look after the property, finances, and general welfare and progress of the village: such as water works, sewers, fire protection, etc.

Who is president of the council?

The mayor.

Who is the chief executive officer?

The mayor.

What are his duties?

It is his duty to see that peace and order prevail in the corporation, to enforce the ordinances, to appoint officers not elected. He must hold court, known as mayor's court, and he has power to try cases.

THE MARSHAL.—What office does a marshal hold in a village.

He is the chief police, and his duties are

similar to those of the chief of police in cities or the sheriff in the county.

CITY.—What is a city?

When a village has grown in population to five thousand or more, by vote of the electors it may become a city.

How are cities divided?

Into two classes, and these classes are divided into grades, and are based upon the population. As the law provides for each grade in the city government, and they differ in different cities in Ohio, we will give but a general outline. Cities are divided into wards, and in most cases the wards are divided into precincts.

What are the officers of a city?

The legislative officers are the city coun- cilmen. The executive officers are a may- or, a marshal, (or chief of police), a solicit- or, a street commissioner and a treasurer. These are elected by the people. The city council elects its own secretary, who is called the city clerk.

THE CITY COUNCIL.—What are its duties.

The duties are similar to the council in a village, but more extensive. In some cities ordinances for the expenditure of money granting a franchise, are submit- ted to the mayor for approval. If vetoed it may pass the council by a vote of two-thirds of the members present. The city council elects its own president.

THE MAYOR.—The duties of the mayor have been described in the village government, except he is not the president of the council, and in some cities he has the veto power; also, if there is a police judge there is no mayor's court.

THE CLERK.—How is the city clerk elected?　　　　　　　　　　　　,

By the council, as the secretary.

What are his duties?

To attend the meetings of the council, to keep a record of all proceedings and of the ordinances passed, and to publish the same. He is the custodian of the records, papers, books ,laws, and ordinances of the city.

THE OTHER CITY OFFICERS.—The treasurer, sometimes called comptroller, or auditor, is the bookkeeper for the city. The solicitor or prosecuting attorney is the legal adviser of the city. Cities are divided into departments, such as finance, law, public safety and public improvements. Of each of these departments the mayor appoints a director. These directors have full charge of their departments.

LECTURES.

CLUBS AND SOCIETIES desiring to secure good lecturers can do so by writing to the following persons:

Mrs. Josephine Woodward, Commercial Tribune, Cincinnati, O.. Subject: "A Correspondent in Cuba."

Mrs. W. J. Huggins, 5 Stewart Ave., Mansfield, Ohio, Subject: "The Rubaiyat of Omar Khayyam."

Mrs. S. M. Perkins, 121 Adelbert Ave., Cleveland, Ohio. Subject: "Margaret Fuller, the Thinker, and Mary Lyon, the Worker."

Miss Frances H. Ensign, Madison, Ohio. Subject: "Queen Esther and Her Mission."

Mrs. W. J. Huggins, 5 Stewart Ave., Mansfield, Ohio, prepares programs and calendars for literary or travelers' clubs; corresponds with club women concerning reference books and articles for club papers, and assists in organizing new clubs.

Mrs. Emma A. Cramner, Aberdeen, South Dakota. Subject: "Woman's Progress vs. the World's Prejudice."

BOOKS THAT EVERY ONE SHOULD HAVE.

American and British Authors, by
Prof. Frank V. Irish...........$1 35
Treasured Thoughts, by Prof. Frank
V. Irish 50
These two books are worth twice the
cost.
Address Prof. F. V. Irish, Columbus, O.

Memories of the Crusade, by Mother
Stewart ....$1.50 and $2.00
The Crusade of Great Britain, by Mother
Stewart $1.00
For a correct history of the Temperance
Crusade, send for these books. Address
Mother Stewart, Springfield, Ohio.

Glimpses of Fifty Years, by Frances E.
Willard, ...$2.00, $2.75 and $3.50
Do Everything, Frances E. Willard. 25
A Great Mother, by Frances E. Wil-
lard 1 50
For the above books address Woman's
Temperance Publishing Association, "The
Temple," Chicago, Ills.

Parliamentary Procedure and Practice,
by John George Bourinot, C. M. G.,
LL. D.

Constitutional History of Canada, by
John George Bourinot.
In the study of Canadian history and
parliamentary proceedings no books are
any better than the above.
Address John George Bourinot, Ottawa
Canada.

"Occupations for Women," by Frances E.
Willard, and "Success," an up-to-date journal of push, principle and progress, with
20th century ideas,both to new subscribers
of "Success" for one year, $2.00.
Address,   SUCCESS COMPANY,
Cooper Union, New York City.

Do You Own

A Compendium
—AND—
Question Book
of Parliamentary Law?

It is just what every person needs in the busy moments of a public meeting. It is arranged for all societies. It is a ready reference manual prepared in the form of questions and answers. It is the cream of all the larger manuals. No member of a society is thoroughly equipped without this work This instructive little book has met with a hearty reception, far beyond our most sanguine expectations. Already the sales have reached seventeen thousand copies. Price, leather, red edges, 40 cents. Leatherette, 25 cents. Published by the author,   LILIAN COLE-BETHEL,

738 E. Long St., Columbus, O.

TESTIMONIALS.

Madam Bethel: San Francisco, Cal.

Each member of your morning class held in the tower room, California Hotel, San Francisco, in May, 1894, had been connected with different organizations for years, had felt her need of parliamentary knowledge, and spent much time digging into the lore of different authors upon this subject, but never, until you taught your comprehensive, clear-cut and sufficient method, could either feel sure of carrying a motion through all its prerogatives without losing her head as well as the motion. No knowledge is more esesntial to active women than Parliamentary Law. It brings out from the folded napkin and mouldy grave her God-given talents; and, dear madame, how better can you help her on to victory and up to the "House of Good" than to impart confidence and power by a thorough knowledge of Parliamentary Law?

Your method is indisputably the best and your Question Book the most helpful. Yours sincerely,

MRS. I. A. CONKLIN.

___

Springfield, O., July 16, 1896.

It gives me great pleasure to commend the course of drills in Parliamentary Usages that Mrs. Lilian Cole-Bethel is so well prepared to give to Women's Clubs and other organizations. Mrs. Bethel is not only well prepared by a thorough knowledge of the subject, but she has the faculty in a rare degree of imparting information. The Women's Clubs of Springfield were enthusiastic over her class methods of teaching and her personal interest in her classes. I wish all the Women's Literary Clubs of Ohio might be fortunate enough to secure her services.

CLEMENTINE B. BUCHWALTER,
Chairman of Correspondence for Ohio of the Gen'l Federation of Woman's Clubs.

Sec'y Com. on Woman's Congresses.

———

Oxford, O., April 25, 1896.

Mrs. Lilian Cole-Bethel gave her series of lessons on Parliamentary Law at the Western College, with very great success. We cordially endorse her work as thorough, comprehensive and exceedingly interesting. It is an especially valuable course of instruction for college men and women.

LEILA S. McKEE,
President Western College, Oxford, Ohio.

———

THE CINCINNATI WOMAN'S CLUB.

The class in Parliamentary Law held in the rooms of the Cincinnati Woman's Club under the auspices of the Alumnae Association of the Western Seminary desire heartily to endorse Mrs. Lilian Cole-Bethel as a teacher and exponent of parliamentary law. She is perfectly conversant with every point connected with her subject and is endowed with that valuable gift so frequently denied teachers, the ability clearly to impart her knowledge. We are certain that we have received a training which will be of permanent value to us all, and hope that at some time in the future, convenient to Mrs. Cole-Bethel, we may have another and an advanced course under her instruction.. By order of the class.

MARGARET C. MOREHEAD,
ELLEN ANDERSON JUDKINS.
KATHERINE HOLIBIRD DUBLE.
Committee.
Cincinnati, Ohio, March 28, 1896.

———

Utica, N. Y., Dec. 6, 1897.
The Oneida Chapter of the Daughters of the American Revolution, after a most profitable and enjoyable series of of lectures by Lilian Cole-Bethel, of Columbus, O., on Parliamentary Law, gladly testify to the abundant satisfaction which Mrs. Bethel gave to all who were so fortunate as to meet and hear her.
E. W. WALCOTT, Regent.
D. J. LINDSLEY.
A. W. CALDER.
L. J. LYNCH,
G. D. CURRAN,
Committee.

———

Illinois Female College,
Jacksonville, Ills., Dec. 16, 1897.
Both teachers and students found pleasure and profit in the visit of Mrs. Lilian Cole-Bethel of Coumbus,Ohio, Nov. 16 to 20, and in the series of Parmentary drills which she conducted. A constantly increasing interest was manifest during the week, and all who attended the drills were impressed with

the necessity of a thorough knowledge of Parliamentary usage. Mrs. Bethel is bright and happy in her work, and makes the exercises entertaining as well as instructive. The series closed with a mock convention, with delegates from all parts of the country, which proved of great interest and profit. We hope that Mrs. Bethel may come back next year.

JOSEPH R. HARKER, President.

Parliamentary Drills.

By Mrs. Lilian Cole-Bethel.

Notice to all societies: Recognizing the importance of familiarity with the rules of usage, I have set apart a portion of my time for giving parliamentary drills. My experience in drill work before audiences from New York to San Francisco enables me to say, any one taking my full course of lessons can easily learn to master the entire subject. The course consists of five lessons with illustrations and practical tests. Send for testimonials and terms to

LILIAN COLE-BETHEL,

738 E. Long St., Columbus, Ohio.

"A Compendium and Question Book of Parliamentary Law," arranged by Lilian Cole-Bethel. This little volume, only about fifty pages in number and small in dimensions—it is what one might term "meaty," since every word in it is worth "inwardly digesting." It is dedicated to womankind and has been especially designed as a hand book that may be relied upon in the study of Parliamentary form. It will be found of great value to W. C. T. U. women, who wish to post themselves thoroughly on the ways and means of entering the "arena of discussion," and becoming victors therein,—The Union Signal, Chicago.

Haines' Falls, N. Y., Sept. 11, 1894.

Mrs. Lilian Cole-Bethel—My Dear Sister: I like your little book so much that I shall carry it with me to Cleveland and I believe that, other things being equal, we ought to use a parliamentary book by a woman in order to encourage the public opinion concerning woman's ability in this direction.

I think it might be well that we make your book our standard. I feel sure it will be of great value to me because it can be so readily referred to, which is of vital importance to any one who is presiding.

Sincerely your friend and comrade,

FRANCES E. WILLARD.

Columbus, O., October 13, 1892.

I have examined with care and pleasure your "Compendium and Question Book of Parliamentary Law," and speak for it a large field of usefuless.

Your mode of presenting parliamentary practice—by questions and answers—so simplifies what is generally difficult, that a novice can soon become proficient and feel at ease in a deliberative society, and confidently take an active part in its proceedings. With kind regards,   ORESTES A. B. SENTER,
Gen'l Grand Master, R. & S. M. of the U. S.

FROM BISHOP VINCENT.
Buffalo, N. Y., Nov. 12, 1892.

I have received and examined with some care your admirable little manual of Parliamentary Law. It deserves a wide sale. It makes a good text book.

Yours truly,

JOHN H. VINCENT.

Ohio Wesleyan University, Delaware, O., Nov. 10, '92.

Thanks for the copy of your Compendium of Parliamentary Law. My hasty examination of it gives me a very favorable impression of the volume. Its clearness and brevity make it an admirable handbook for a busy president. Sincerely yours,

J. W. BASHFORD, Pres't.

Kansas City, Mo., Dec. 5, 1892.

I have received your book on Parliamentary Usage, and have looked it over and find it good and thoroughly practical. I like your dedication. Your "Hints in Behalf of Public Speakers" should be printed in silver and framed in gold. Altogether it is the most thoroughly helpful book along the lines of public meetings and deliberative bodies that I have ever

seen. 1 shall carry it around with me until I have learned it all. CLARA C. HOFFMAN,
State President Missouri W. C. T. U.

Guilford College, N. C., Nov. 18, 1892.

I consider your book the most helpful in the session of convention of anything I have seen. It is very thorough and correct and shows a complete mastery of the intricate subject of parliamentary law by its author. Yours truly,
MARY C. WOODY,
State President N. C. W. C. T. U.

MEDAL CONTESTS.

If you want to replenish your treasuries and at the same time disseminate Gospel Temperance and Prohibition, hold a W. C. ˙ T. U. or Demorest Medal Contest. These popular entertainments are not confined to temperance organizations, but are being held by young people's church societies, schools, colleges, etc. Send a two-cent stamp to Mrs. A. E. Carmen, National Superintendent Contest Work, The Temple, Chicago, Ill., for circulars, rules and prices of books and medals. Miss Willard says: "We are fortunate in our superintendent of contest work, Mrs. Carmen, who is capable, devoted, and gives her entire time to the work. The encouragement she has received from Madame Demorest, and the confidence shown her by placing that work in her care will strengthen the hands of our superintendent. I rejoice this honor has been shown her." Write to

MRS. A. E. CARMEN,
The Temple, Chicago, Ill.

www.ingramcontent.com/pod-product-compliance
Lightning Source LLC
Chambersburg PA
CBHW020111030726
47498CB00006B/2058